"Yes, and I have the story in my room. Do you want to read it?"

Landries gave a short laugh, almost a snort.

"That is a dumb question, Goldman. You know that I would travel halfway around the world to read his story. But doesn't it exhaust you to be the sounding board for him? How can you stand living through all his pain, his suffering and disappointments?"

Goldman shook his head. "I don't know, but I have to finish what we started. It's like being hooked on drugs. I have to complete it, and the worst of it is, I know that I never will. He has outlived the Roman Empire, the Persian and British Empires and I see no indicator that he will not outlive the both of us—that is, unless the Second Coming of Christ arrives sooner than we expect . . ."

In the cab, and in spite of himself, Landries opened the manuscript and peeked at the cover to see the title. Perhaps it would give him a clue as to Casca's location in this particular segment of his history. His eyes fell upon it—

Casca, The Persian. . . .

Other Ace Charter Titles By Barry Sadler:

CASCA: THE ETERNAL MERCENARY
CASCA: GOD OF DEATH
CASCA: THE WAR LORD
CASCA: PANZER SOLDIER
CASCA: THE BARBARIAN

CASCA: THE PERSIAN
#6

BARRY SADLER

CHARTER
NEW YORK

A DIVISION OF CHARTER COMMUNICATIONS INC.
A GROSSET & DUNLAP COMPANY

51 Madison Avenue
New York, New York 10010

CASCA #6: THE PERSIAN
Copyright © 1982 by Barry Sadler
All rights reserved. No part of this book may be reproduced in any form or by any means, except for the inclusion of brief quotations in a review, without permission in writing from the publisher.

All characters in this book are fictitious. Any resemblance to actual persons, living or dead, is purely coincidental.

An Ace Charter Original.

First Ace Charter Printing May 1982
Published simultaneously in Canada
Manufactured in the United States of America

2 4 6 8 0 9 0 7 5 3 1

CASCA: THE PERSIAN

PROLOGUE

Julius Goldman wandered among the booths and stands of the purveyors of medical supplies and goods. Stethoscopes and enema kits mingled with the latest in medical technology, while machines that could represent a three-dimensional scan of the human body were displayed alongside films demonstrating the use of laser beams to seal off tiny bleeders in the eyes.

This annual gathering of the American Medical Association was always interesting and exciting to him. He knew many of those present and a lot of them were close colleagues, but Goldman's eyes were searching for one face in particular.

He finally found him in the maze of booths and slick presentations. He was leaning over the counter of one of the booths talking to one of the bright-faced, pretty young girls, hired to attract the attentions of the doctors to a particular booth.

Goldman worked his way through the crowd and touched the man he'd been looking for on the shoulder.

"Doctor Landries?"

The former Army colonel, and Goldman's onetime commanding officer, turned around. He was still tanned and lean, extraordinarily healthy looking. His hair was thinner now and completely silver, but his eyes and manner were quick and sure as ever; so was his grasp of Goldman's hand in a sincere display of pleasure at seeing his old comrade again. He laughed pleasantly.

"Goldman! The Hebraic hero of the Eighth Field Hospital, and terror of all nurses. How in the hell are you, son?"

He took Goldman's arm, completely forgetting the sweet young thing he'd been talking to. She was pouting a bit now, Goldman could see, at losing the attention of Bob Landries, but another, younger neurosurgeon was moving in to replace him.

He guided Goldman out of the convention center and they boarded one of the buses that made regular runs to the hotels servicing the center.

Goldman was genuinely happy at seeing his friend again. It had been a long time. Landries ran his hand through his thinning hair and looked out the window of the bus, watching the streets of Atlanta pass by as they pulled on to Peachtree, heading to the downtown area.

"Have you heard any more about our mutual friend?"

Goldman knew who Landries was talking about. He smoothed down the vest of his conservative three-piece pinstripe suit, a little uncomfortable at the tightness of the vest at the midriff. He would have to lose some weight.

"Yes!" He started to continue but Landries stopped him.

"Wait until we get to the hotel. We'll settle down with a drink and talk. I always have a need for one when the name of Casey Romain comes up."

Goldman agreed and the two talked of things doctors talk about: new techniques, prices for services, and, naturally, the good old days when they were some years younger.

Landries was seven years Goldman's senior, but looked about the same age, with his tanned face and lean body. He'd always been an exercise nut, Goldman remembered, feeling a little guilty at letting himself go to pot over the past few years. After looking at his old boss he made himself a promise —knowing he more than likely would not keep it— that he would try and put himself back into shape.

Taking their turn, they exited the bus and entered the air-conditioned enclosure of the hotel. It was a modern inn with elevators of glass chutes and an open-air restaurant and lounge in the lobby. They found a table with a degree of privacy beside an indoor pond where goldfish swam with studied unconcern.

Drinks were ordered. Landries, as usual, had a double Blackjack and water; Goldman ordered Scotch and soda. The two men waited until their drinks were served and their waitress with the airline smile had left them before they commenced talking about that which both knew was the main reason for their meeting.

Goldman began first, after taking a sip of his drink.

"Casca . . . or Casey, as you and I knew him . . ."

The names called to Landries' memory the time

they'd first met the man Romain, who'd been brought to them as a casualty in Vietnam. Goldman continued his story, and Bob Landries was slightly envious that Casca had chosen Goldman to tell his story to. But then Goldman had been the one who'd spotted the strange healing process of a wound that should have been fatal, and had heard the beginnings of the weird tale of the man who'd killed Jesus at Golgotha, and of the punishment that Jesus had given him. To wander the earth unable to die until the Second Coming, forever a soldier—condemned to a life of endless wandering and war. He smiled a little, recalling how he and Goldman had had the man's medical records destroyed after Casca, or Casey, had disappeared from the hospital. No one would have believed them.

A few years after the Vietnam debacle had ended, their patient had shown up at Goldman's house and begun telling him the full story of his odyssey through the ages. He had the power to take Goldman into his life and enable him to experience all that he had done. Since then, Goldman had developed a compulsion to put down the words and story of Casca Rufio Longinus, soldier of Imperial Rome, whose travels and adventures over the face of the earth made the journey of Ulysses seem no more than a mild weekend excursion in the country.

Landries half emptied his glass and called for another. He coughed, clearing his throat.

"I suppose the reason you came to this gathering of the entire medical world is that you've had another visit from our friend?"

Goldman nodded his head in the affirmative. "Yes, and I have the story in my room. Do you want to read it?"

Landries gave a short laugh, almost a snort.

"That is a dumb question, Goldman. You know that I would travel halfway around the world to read his story. But doesn't it exhaust you to be the sounding board for him? How can you stand living through all his pain, his suffering and disappointments?"

Goldman shook his head. "I don't know, but I have to finish what we started. It's like being hooked on drugs. I have to complete it, and the worst of it is, I know that I never will. He has outlived the Roman Empire, the Persian and British Empires and I see no indicator that he will not outlive the both of us—that is, unless the Second Coming of Christ arrives sooner than we expect." Meeting Casca had left Goldman with a few questions. He was fast doubting the teachings of his faith about Jesus not being the Son of God. He continued.

"Let's finish these and go up to my room. I'll give you the manuscript to take back to your own room and read."

Landries agreed and paid their tab. They took one of the glass-cocooned elevators up to Goldman's room. Inside, Goldman handed the manuscript to Landries and they returned to the lobby. He escorted Landries to the doorway, where the heat of the Atlanta streets was being restrained outside.

Landries was anxious to get started on the reading of the next story of Casca and asked Goldman,

"Where is he this time?"

Goldman smiled. "Be patient, Bob. After all, Casca has been patient for years, hasn't he?"

Landries agreed, and after he'd made Goldman promise to mail him all the manuscripts from there on, they shook hands and said goodbye.

Landries exited the hotel into the midday heat, hailing a cab to return him to his own hotel. He didn't feel like waiting for the buses that came by every thirty minutes. He had to get back, relax, and see what had happened to Casca.

In the cab, and in spite of himself, he opened the manuscript and peeked at the cover to see the title. Perhaps it would give him a clue as to Casca's location in this particular segment of his history. His eyes fell upon it—

CASCA, The Persian. . . .

ONE

Hot, boiling, shimmering, the sun broke over the rim of the world, sending spears of flaming light across the clear skies of the high steppes. By midday it would be hot enough to cook a brain in its own pan. But for now there was still enough chill left over from the night air to make the breath of the horse and its rider visible in the small clouds of vapor that were whisked away by the freshening morning breeze.

That cool breeze would soon change into a moisture-sucking blast furnace. Before then, the man and his horse would have to find shelter, as had the snakes and lizards. Shelter from the killing rays of the life-giving and -taking sun of high Asia.

To the west, the lifeless, barren, sky-reaching peaks known as the roof of the world, with their eternal caps of ice and gale-swept snow, seemed terribly distant and aloof from the sufferings of those who ventured to cross the desolate wastes of the desert in its shadow.

The rider raised his eyes, red-rimmed and sore from the ever-present grains of sand that invaded every pore and opening of his body, and even the food he ate. He understood now why the men of this region's tribes nearly always had their teeth worn down to stubs before their beards turned gray.

There was sand in everything they ate from the time of their birth to their death. Every day the grit ground their teeth down a little more until there was nothing left but smooth stubs resting against the gums. The thought of it made his own teeth ache.

His horse stumbled, then caught itself on wobbly legs. It scarcely resembled the fine-blooded, pampered animal it had been when Sung mi Hsiung, the commander of the garrison at the Jade Gate, had given it to him. Its rider was scarcely in any better condition. His posture told of the weary, lonely miles they had come. He doubted that if he tried to trade in the animal right now, he could receive even a couple of sick goats in exchange.

But they had come far from the wall that runs forever. He had chosen not to take the Suget pass trail back to the Capital of Kushan on the banks of the Indus. No, this time he followed the silk road, but now was the wrong time for such a crossing. The last two waterholes had been dry; even when he dug down a depth of several feet he could find no trace of moisture.

The rider raised his eyes to the sky, the pale blue of them almost washed out by the gray of the dawn. Deep lines crinkled at the edges of them gave him a slightly Oriental look. From a distance, he could have passed for a nomadic tribesman as the skin that was exposed was as dark as a mongol's.

Nowhere had he heard such silence as that of this region of the great wastes, where it was said, made on the winds was the howling of the lost souls, as dunes of sand were shifted from one spot to another, one grain at a time. For months, that was the only sign of movement until the wind demons came in their full fury. The force of the wind, carrying the sand with it in sky-darkening clouds, would strip the flesh from a man's body in a few minutes and leave nothing but bare bones and rags as silent testimony to the vengeance of the wind demons.

The lands of Chin lay a thousand and more miles behind him. He had lived there longer than he had in any other place in his life and felt as if he were leaving a part of him behind. But his own personal demon was driving him, back to the land of his birth, back to Rome.

For all of his life, he had thought that Rome was the center of the world and the only real barrier against the hordes of barbarism. But in the lands behind the Great Wall, he had found out that in comparison to the culture and refinements of Chin, Rome itself was only a few steps ahead of the barbarians. Still, Rome was the place of his birth and sometimes, no matter how a man may have been treated, he has to go back to his source. He was still Casca Rufio Longinus, a soldier and sometimes even a slave of the Empire.

Ahead of him, he knew, still lay the lands of Sogdiana and Parthia, which he would have to pass through before reaching the first of the Roman *cominions*. Parthia! It still held a bitter taste for him. He had fought there under the Eagles of

Avidius Cassius and participated in the sacking of the city of Cestiphon—where forty-five thousand had died in one day.

Pulling his horse to a stop, he dismounted, took the reins, and led the animal to a cluster of tall brush and withered, leafless trees. There he carefully doled out a slim measure of his precious water supply to wipe the muzzle and moisten the delicate membranes of the horse's nostrils to keep them from bleeding. A handful for the horse to taste, and he licked the remaining moisture from his own fingers, careful to waste nothing. Taking what had once been a fine cloak of red silk, he spread it over the branches of the withered trees to make a sheltered spot to protect them from the sun that would soon be over them.

Placing the horse where he could have some benefit from their meager shelter, he stripped down to the skin in order to shake out his tunic and the loose trousers he wore. His body was crisscrossed with uncounted scars of various degrees of severity. Some he had received as a slave in the war galleys of Rome, others came from battles he now found hard to recall.

When he was satisfied that he had shaken out most of the sand that had managed to creep into every seam and wrinkle, he redressed himself, wincing at the raw spots in his groin and armpits. Lying down, he tried to make himself as comfortable as possible moving several rocks from under tender spots. But his leg had an ache in it. A dull, burning throb where a brass arrow head was imbedded deep in the muscles of his left thigh. A souvenir from a Parthian marksman at Cestiphon.

Closing his eyes, he tried to rest, ignoring the labored breathing of his horse. If they didn't come to water soon the horse would die, and that meant he would walk, for Mithra only knew how many miles until he could steal or buy another one. As far as horses dying, that didn't particularly concern him. At least he'd have some fresh meat and the blood would give him strength. The Romans were practical people, not given to an excess of sentiment.

As he slept, the heat of the day grew in intensity. Hot and dry, it sucked the moisture from his skin as fast as it appeared, leaving only traces of his body salts behind to streak his tunic. Flies buzzed in frustration as they tried to beat the sun to the life-giving moisture that came from his pores. Flies, it seemed, were the only creatures in existence that could appear from nowhere, in a hellhole such as this where even the lizards buried themselves in the sand to escape the heat.

Semiconscious, he would sweep them away from his face and eyes, then turn and dream of places and people long dead, faces of those he had loved and of those he had killed. They came in a jumbled torrent until all merged together and he couldn't tell them apart.

His horse hung its head low and tried to sleep also, tail twitching from side to side, shivers running up its flanks. It too tried to shake off the nagging dronc of the flies. As these two tossed and squirmed in their restless sleep, others were awake and moving. Two forces of men were converging on a waterhole some twenty miles in front. Each unaware of the other, they followed separate trails. Both parties had the look of hard men about them.

Those from the south were led by a slender warrior with his head shaved bald except for a long scalplock. He was the youngest of the warriors in whose bloodlines showed some trace of the west. Several had fair hair and light-colored eyes. The other party coming from the north was made up of short, stocky men whose faces had been seared with red hot irons at the moment of their birth, so that only mustaches grew on their lips and nothing at all on their chins. These riders' legs were twisted and deformed from the years they had spent on horseback. The bows they carried were made of laminated wood and horn, similar to those of the Parthians. One thing they had that was different from those coming from the south: they had not just the look of men who killed, but men who lusted after it. *Huns!* Those nomadic tribesmen worshipped the primal spirits of the earth and sky and prayed before a naked sword.

They would meet those from the south at the waterhole and when they did, men would die, for the Huns and the men of Kushan were blood enemies and had been so for five hundred years.

Casca, former Baron of Chin, used his saddlebags for a pillow. The fortune in gems, given to him by the Emperor Tzin as a parting gift, gave him small comfort. At that moment he would have traded them all for a full goatskin of rancid swamp water. Moving, he tried to find a more comfortable position as his purse dug into his groin. The irritating object inside the leather pouch was his seal of office. The Chu *hou wang* of a noble of the court of the Son of Heaven; a solid gold seal, with a rounded knob of tortoise shell. This seal was what he had needed to gain horses, food, and lodging while in the lands of Chin. But here it was just as useless as the gems in his saddlebags.

The short double-edged sword close to his hand was infinitely more valuable than either the gems or the seal, at least until he reached lands civilized enough to appreciate the value of the small collection of rainbows that rested under his brown shaggy-haired head.

Several times he would wake for a few heat-drugged moments, then drop back off into his uneasy slumber. Not until the sun began its decline did he finally stir himself to rising. Taking a double handful of dried mare's milk curds, he mixed them with enough water to soften them and give the illusion of wetness. He ate one handful and fed the rest to his horse as he watched the heat waves dance and shimmer over the floor of the desert.

That night, as he led his horse over the sands, he looked to the skies and the twinkling, distant stars. It was said in Chin that the astronomers there had charted the courses of over eleven thousand of the sparkling lights. To what purpose, he really didn't understand, but those distant lights were as important to them as were their gods. It was said that they could tell the future from them. But if they could, he couldn't see how man could keep screwing things up—especially if he knew beforehand what was going to happen.

As the constellation known as The Hunter passed overhead, he came across the mummified remains of a camel and its rider, lying side by side on the trail. The skin of the man was drawn tight in a perpetual leathery sneer, the lips pulled back from the teeth. Here, not even the vultures ventured to clean up. The packs on the camel had already been opened and picked over so Casca didn't bother. Others had come this way since the unknown traveler had died. It could have been a month or even several years ago. It didn't matter to him and certainly not to the dessicated husk lying there.

The warriors of Kushan had reached the waterhole as Casca passed the dead man and the camel. They were lying now, drinking, face down in the murky waters of the spring-fed refuge. From a nearby hill, a lone horseman watched them. The Hun disappeared back into the darkness to rejoin his gnomish comrades.

There was not room for both groups at the oasis and the Huns were not known for sharing anything, even if the Kushanites would have been so inclined, which was not likely.

A hundred times since passing through the Jade Gate, Casca had cursed himself for leaving behind him the silken pavilions and comforts of Chin. He could have waited a little longer before leaving, but smartass that he was, he had to try a crossing at this time. Before dawn he made camp once more, this time in a cluster of boulders. The ground had become rougher, but at least he knew that he was leaving the sands behind him. From his map he knew that the waterhole was not far ahead. He would rest a little while in the shade of the rocks and then move on and try to reach it before the next nightfall. He didn't want to take a chance on passing it in the dark.

The Huns had moved in closer to the waterhole and were preparing for the slaughter. They took strips of leather to cover their horses' hooves, to muffle even more the slight sounds made by their unshod hooves as they crossed over the rocky ground leading to the oasis in the rocks.

Half their number had dismounted and now moved on twisted legs to vantage points in the rocks, where they would take easy shots with their bows at the targets below them.

Exhausted, the Kushanites slept. The four sentries on watch at the entrance to the spring also fell into a deep, deep sleep, heads nodding. It was to be a sleep from which they would never wake. The young leader of the Kushanites would have had their heads if he had known of their dereliction. He was of the tribe of the Yueh Chih and had more of the blood of Asia in his veins. But this night he slept deeply, wrapped in his horse blanket and unaware of the death that was slowly approaching.

The Hunnish bowmen waited until the two Kushanite sentries were taken out, their throats slit with skinning knives, then they drew back the strings and targeted the sleeping bodies below. Their targets were easy to mark in the glow of the campfire by the dark waters of the spring.

A half-dozen arrows found their way into the backs and stomachs of the sleeping warriors before one managed a scream of agony. The rest leapt to their feet, weapons at the ready, only to be trod down under the muffled hooves of the Huns' war horses. Heads fell to the ground to lie grinning obscenely by the rocks, as the bodies they had just recently been so attached to jerked and twitched, heels drumming against the hard earth.

The young warrior of the Yueh Chih managed to sink his sword into the chest of one Hun's horse, sending it and its rider crashing to the ground, where he dispatched the seared face of the barbarian with a well-aimed stroke of his *yatagai*. His victory yell was short-lived as a thrown ax struck with the flat of its blade, sending him back into the darkness he had so recently come out of. The rest of his band died where they stood, no survivors. Prisoners were a luxury the Huns could ill afford at this time. They had been ordered to make all haste to the felt yurts of the tribes gathering far to the east, where there was to be a great killing. They had been driven far from the Great Wall by the armies of Chin, but now they were coming back in greater numbers than ever before and the wall would not long stand between them and riches of Chin.

Their only survivor was spared for the moment. The Hun leader wished to question him as to the reason warriors of Kushan were so far from their borders. But until the young warrior regained consciousness, he was of little use. Meanwhile, his captors helped themselves to whatever they liked from the packs and bodies of the dead. They slit the throat of one of the Kushan horses and soon had the rich red flesh sizzling over hot coals.

Casca raised his face and sniffed the wind. Meat, freshly cooking meat! His mouth tried to salivate and failed; there was too little moisture in his system to waste for such luxuries. Tying his animal's reins to a bush, he readied himself to see just who it was that was having a hot meal. In this region, it was not probable that he would be made welcome. Loosening his blade in its scabbard, he then strung his bow, grunting from the effort to bend it down to where he could slip the gut string on it. The bow was a gift from Sung Ti the Baron of Chung Wei, made years ago when they had fought the Mongols and Huns together in the service of the Son of Heaven. Less than four feet long when strung, the bow, made in Hunnish manner, could drive an arrow through the side of a horse and still have enough power to kill a man on the other side.

Making his way cautiously through the boulders and scrub brush, he came upon the signs left by the Huns. There were at least ten of them, maybe more. Snaking his way closer to the smell of roasting meat, he crested a small rise and looked down on the spring.

Whistling between his teeth, he counted them. Eleven Huns lay about the hole in various states of stupor. They had gorged themselves on red meat and fermented mare's milk. The bodies of the Kushanites had been dragged off to the side and piled in a heap. There, they served to keep the flies off the Huns and on the dead, where even now the insects clustered in black, moving clots on the still-draining bodies.

Casca started to move back and away, content to leave them the waterhole until they finished and moved on. The odds were they wouldn't stay there very long. As he started to crawl back on his belly, a movement in the pile of bodies caught his attention. One wasn't dead. He watched as the figure twisted and tried to sit up, arms and feet bound with strips of rawhide. Something about the man stopped him from retreating. The way he held his head, the set of the jaw, something? Then it came to him. Jugotai! Jugotai, the youngster who had been his guide when he first came to the east from across the mountains. From this distance it was hard to be certain but it damned sure looked like him, and those *were* Kushanite dead stacked up down there. It bothered him, because the young man down there could not be old enough to have been his guide. That had been nearly thirty years ago. Sighing deeply, he grunted. "Well, if that's the way of it, I might as well get started."

He laid his quiver of arrows beside him and looked over the situation again. Not so good; there were still a lot of Huns down there, and while he might get three or four before the rest got up and moving, it was still risky.

No, he'd have to do something really dirty to get the boy free. Allright, first off I have to reduce the odds a bit, he thought. From where he was perched, there was only one exit for the Huns to take on horseback. All the horses were tied in a line near some dry brush they had been feeding on. There's only one thing that Huns really hate to do, and that is to walk. There were sixteen horses, counting those of the Kushanites. Casca doubted that he would have time to kill them and handle the Huns too! Besides, he wasn't an expert marksman. He could hit the broad side of the target usually, but nothing fancy. The Huns were heavy into sleep. When they awoke, they would have some bad heads from the fermented mare's milk. He knew from personal experience the aftereffects of a night of drinking Kvass. Taking a thatch of dry grass, he pulled some threads from his tunic, tied the grass around the shafts of two arrows, and then laid out the rest of the shafts on the ground, close at hand. The horses were only about one hundred feet away so he wouldn't have any trouble hitting the brush beside them, and, as dry as it was, it should catch on fire pretty fast and still leave him enough time to shoot down at least a couple from the back while they were still sleeping. He struck off a spark from his flint and tinder, blowing it into a small smokeless flame, and touched off the fire arrows. Quickly he sighted, rose to his knees, and drew the cord almost to his ear, letting fly first one, then the other. The twanging of the bow wasn't loud enough to be heard.

The arrows smoked their way into the brush where the horses were tied. As he expected, it didn't take but a few seconds before the brush burst into a rapidly burning flame. The horses shied away from the licking flames and Casca picked new targets. A snoring, sleeping Hun. This time he drew the string all the way back to his ear and the arrow pinned the sleeping man to the earth. He got off two more shots before the whinnying of the horses, combined with the screaming of one of the Huns he had shot, roused the rest of the sleepers. They stumbled to their feet, red-eyed and hung over, reaching for their weapons in confusion. He shot another in the groin, the flat-bladed arrow taking off one testicle.

"Shit," he cursed. He had been aiming at the man's stomach. The horses broke and began to shy away from the flames, but they weren't running. So he took the time to send a couple of shafts into the nearest of the animals' rear ends. This served to give the rest of them the needed impetus to break and run, as did the Huns on their twisted legs, looking for cover and trying to locate their enemy. Casca took one more out with a lucky shot that hit the man squarely between the shoulder blades and exited at hands-length out the front of his chest. By then, he'd had to dodge a couple of arrows himself. He had the advantage of being on the high ground or they probably would have nailed him right off. They were, he admitted, all damned better bowmen than he was.

Yelling down to them, he spoke in the language of Chin. One called back to him, "What is it that you want and who are you that hides from us like a *pariah* dog? Come down and fight."

Casca grinned, his eyes never leaving the Huns in the rocks. "I'm glad to see at least one of you has the ability to speak in more than grunts, grunts that are the natural tongue of your tribes. What I want is to make a deal."

The Hun leader yelled back. "I'm listening."

"Unless you bowlegged little bastards would be fond of walking out of this place and across the desert, I would suggest that you give my offer careful consideration."

"Why should we listen to you? We have you outnumbered and it would be just a matter of time before you're laid out to be properly butchered."

"Normally, that would be true, you ugly little bastard, but not right now. If you won't deal with me, then I'm going to leave you here, take my horse, and go after yours and kill them all. That will guarantee that you will leave your bones on the trail with no one to sing your death song except the flies."

The Huns below realized that what he said was true. He would have the advantage and from what he had just done, there was no doubt that he would do exactly as he said. And it was a long way to the felt yurts of their tribes.

"What is your offer?"

"Let the captive go. Give him a full skin of water and another of good food from his own supplies. Once he is in the clear, we'll leave. Your horses will return before long. They have to come back to drink sometime so you'll just have to wait a little while for them. By then I'll be long gone and you can continue your journey with more horses then you started with. Is that fair enough?"

The Hun below thought about it for a moment. He really had no other choice. "So be it. We'll let you have the Yueh Chih pup and the water and food. But no weapons for him. That would increase your advantage too much."

"I agree," called back Casca. "Send him on up."

Keeping a wary eye on the rocks, one of the Huns slid and waddled over to the Yueh Chih warrior and freed him from his bonds. The young man had heard all that had transpired between the Huns and his hidden ally in the rocks above. He wasted no time in getting a skin of water and a sack of food from the pile of looted goods. He looked longingly at his personal weapons but made no move towards them. Throwing his load on his shoulders, he rapidly began to climb up to his protector's perch. A scarred hand reached out to help and pulled him up to safety. A strong shove and he was clear of the ledge.

Casca gave a curt, "Get your ass to the back and down the ridge. I have a horse there. Give him some water and we'll get our butts out of here while we have the chance." He called back to the Huns, "Now, you girls just be patient. If I see just one inch of your scabby hides away from the waterhole, I'll kill the horses."

He backed away, still careful not to give the Huns a bow shot. By the time he'd made his way back to his horse the young warrior had allowed the animal to sip a large measure of their water supply, and the fluid already had imparted a little life to his lackluster eyes. But it still lacked the strength to carry a double load, so they moved out on foot. Casca leading, they half-walked, half-trotted away from the hole, following the tracks of the panicked horses. After about an hour, and another dose of water followed with a handful of grain from the food sack, Casca's horse was ready to be ridden, but still only by one. The youngster held onto the tail and they were still moving in this manner when they came on the first of the horses resting in the shade of some boulders. The Yueh Chih warrior gave a low whistle and the beast stayed put until the young man gained its reins. It was his own horse. As the youngster swung up into his saddle, Casca asked him, "What is your name? It wouldn't be Jugotai by any chance?"

The youngster whipped his head around, the scalplock flying. "No, I am Shuvar, son of Jugotai. Do you know my father?"

Casca laughed a deep chuckle. "Aye, boy, I

knew him when he was no older than you, many years ago."

The two rode together, rounding up all the horses they could find. Two mounts evaded them but they moved on, herding the horses before them. Shuvar questioned Casca, "Aren't you going to leave them for the Huns as you promised?"

Casca shook his shaggy head. "No way. We missed two and I hate to leave them behind. One thing you learn in life, if you live as long as I have, and that is to never give a barbarian an even break. If we let them get back their mounts they would come after us, or go and kill someone else. Besides, they still have a chance to survive."

When they made camp that night, Shuvar responded to Casca's questions about his reasons for being so far from Kushan's borders. Shuvar told him he was to deliver a message to Chin that they had word the Huns were on the march again. The hordes were gathering together with new allies, including the Mongol tribes, for an all-out assault on Chin. For a while Casca thought about returning with Shuvar, but decided to go on his way. There would be little he could do now and the wheel of time had turned too far for him to go back. With the dawn he bid farewell to Shuvar, gave him his bow and his remaining arrows, three of the horses, and most of the supplies. He would be closer to a place to replenish them than would be the dashing young warrior, who would be crossing the hell that Casca had just traversed.

The youngster wheeled his animals around for the long journey to the first imperial outposts at Ho-T'ien. Before the youngster left he cried out, "I forgot to ask your name, to tell my father who it was that saved his son."

The scar-faced man smiled broadly. "Tell him it was the Roman, Casca, who still lives and walks the earth."

Shuvar's mouth dropped in astonishment. "Hail, Roman! My father told me of your journeys together. But I thought you would surely be a much older man."

The Roman laughed again. "I am young, Shuvar, I am."

"Ride fast and ride well."

Casca waved his sword arm in salute and turned to herd his share of the horses on down the trail leading to Sogdiania and Parthia.

TWO

A week after leaving Shuvar he crossed the Jaxartes river, still keeping to the north of Sogdiana's boundaries. Not until he reached the Oxus did he encounter patrols of armored men. These he gave a wide berth to, staying to himself.

From an occasional caravan he'd heard of the state of the world as they knew it. The Sassanids, he learned, had risen to new heights of power. Since they had replaced the Parthian Kings, their empire had made almost a complete return to a pure Persian influence, though they still made use of the *Cataphracti* and the heavy infantry of their predecessors.

Shuvar had not had time to tell him that even Kushan was under the sovereignty of the Sassanid King and though it was still ruled in his name, it yet paid tribute and recognized the Persians as its overlords.

It was necessary that Kushan have strong allies. The pressure of the Huns was becoming so great that they could not live long and survive without them, and it was better to bow to the Persians than to be beheaded by the Huns.

The Persian soldiery that he did meet had paid little attention to him. As a lone rider he posed no threat to them nor to the Empire. As far as they were concerned he was most obviously not a Hun, and dressed as poorly as he was, in rags, he could not be of much importance to anyone. They had ridden on, ignoring him.

When he reached the city of Nev-Shapur, named after the founder of the new Persian Empire, Shapur II, he hesitated a bit before entering through the protected gates and past the watchful eyes of the bearded sentries. It was the morning rush hour, when the workers of the fields and the merchants from surrounding villages brought their wares into the city proper for sale, or to be transshipped to other parts of the Persian Empire and even to Rome. As the city was located directly on what was known as the silk road, that in itself was enough to guarantee its success as a trading center, and today it was booming as such.

Casca had followed a caravan of double-humped camels, braying and spitting under the loads they carried swinging on their backs. The gates of the city closed at dusk and did not reopen until the first light, and at that time, as it was now, hundreds waited outside the city to gain entry. Most waited within a mile of the city gates, where a place was set aside for them to gather and wait for the coming of the light of *Ahura-mazda,* the sun.

Wending his way through the throngs, he entered the gates without being challenged. The city was much the same as many others he'd been in; the myriad smells and the crying of the vendors to sell their wares, all in a dozen tongues. The city itself was clean, but architecturally was different from Rome.

Since the Sassanids had taken over, he could see that they'd done their best to bring back the ways of their age; the buildings and official structures showed the influence of centuries long past. Bas-relief carvings were to be seen everywhere—scenes reflecting the great triumphs of Persia's past and, even more, of its new era.

Casca found his way to the street set aside for the jewelers and money lenders. He was careful not to use any language but Latin. From the friezes he had seen, representing Shapur accepting the surrender of the Roman emperor, Valerian, he figured Romans were not welcome. Valerian had died while still a captive of the Persian who led him through the principal cities of his lands on a leash, crawling before his captors, the Persian hosts, on his belly. The descriptiveness of the friezes was explicit. In Rome Constantine was emperor, but from the vibrance of these Persians, Casca figured Rome had better watch its ass if they ever decided to move west.

A traveler pointed him in the direction of a brick building said to be the residence of a money lender and jeweler, but only after wrinkling his nose in distaste at the sour odor coming from the light-eyed stranger in the rags of a beggar. He did comment, however, on Casca's fine horse.

Entering the confines of the cool building, his eyes went blank for a second before adjusting themselves to the darkness inside. A figure emerged from behind a multicolored curtain and looked questioningly at him. He inquired first in

Aramaic, which Casca didn't speak, then looked closer at the square-muscled frame with the light eyes and sun-bleached hair. Could he be a Circassian? No, there was something about this stranger in his shop that made him think not.

"*Vale*, Roman. What do you here in the city of Shapur? Perhaps you seek your death? If so, it will be easy to find, if those outside see you as I do."

A larger figure loomed behind the shopkeeper; a massive man with shaven head and huge arms that looked long enough to reach to his knees. Casca sized up what he assumed was the shopkeeper's bodyguard. He appeared big enough to mate with one of the sculptures of bulls he'd seen that appeared life-sized in glazed bricks on the city walls.

The bodyguard looked Casca over, too, while Casca was deciding that the merchant was not of the race of the Aryan Persians. He gave the gray-haired, full-bearded shopkeeper a shock, then, speaking in the man's native tongue.

"*Shalom*, son of David. We are both a long way from our homelands, so it seems."

Shopkeeper Samuel Ben Ezra hesitated in surprise. Not many in these lands spoke the tongue of Solomon. He looked again at his guest with suspicion.

"*Shalom*, and peace unto you, Roman. How may I serve you in my humble establishment?"

Casca removed his pouch from the waistband and took out two large yellow sapphires. He placed them softly into the hand of the Jew.

"Give me what is fair in silver and gold for these stones."

Samuel held the stones to the light, moving closer to the door of his shop to take best advantage of the sun. He turned them over and over.

"What do you want for these?"

Casca smiled. "I said give me what is fair. Surely you would not cheat a fellow stranger who is as far from his home as you are. I know your people and know that their word is their bond. Tell me what you will give. It shall be fair and I will accept it."

Samuel pursed his lips in wonder. This was a strange one. But, he was right. The Jewish merchants of the world survived only because their word was good, and all who traded with them knew it. A letter from one merchant to another promising payment in gold or silver to the bearer would be honored by any of his race as far away as the limits of the known world, and without question.

The Jewish merchants of the world survived because of this fact, and though the nations of the world might be enemies, the business of commerce had to go on. Even though the Jews had been persecuted and driven from their homelands, they were the only ones who could fill this gap and this everyone knew. Commerce was the key to survival for the sons of David and if they were to ever break their word, the blood of their people would flow again and they would have no place left on this earth. So, by necessity, they had become the bankers of the world. With no nation to call their own, they were bound only by their loyalty to one another and the oaths to their trade.

"I will give you twenty silver coins of Darius and one-half gold denarius of Rome."

Casca extended his hand to shake. "It is done."

The business settled, the two men went to Samuel's private quarters. Drinks of mint were served by his bodyguard, who watched over the old man like a mother hen, reluctant to leave his master even when Samuel dismissed him with instructions to return to the front of the shop to keep an eye on his goods.

The two men sat across from each other, Casca commenting on the softness of the cushions they sat on as compared to his saddle. Their drinks sat on a low table of inlaid teak and enamel mosaic. Samuel served bread and salt. The two tasted as one and the bond was made.

"Welcome to my house and the blessing of The Lord be with you. Forgive me now if I repeat myself, but in this land you are in more danger than myself. Rome and its people are not loved here. I would suggest that you go on your way and leave the nation of Shapur behind as swiftly as your legs, or those of your horse, will carry you. If you have need of transport, I can arrange for you to join a caravan whose master owes me a personal favor."

Casca nodded, sipped his hot mint, and replied:

"I am not in as much danger as you may believe. I bear letters from the Son of Heaven, the Emperor of Chin. As you surely know, messengers are given favored status by all civilized nations and must be treated with courtesy. There is really no danger for me here. I do plan to return to my lands soon, but the trail over the silk road is long and I am tired and would rest here a while before continuing my journey. Speaking of rest, could you recommend an inn? One that is outside the gates for the time being. I wish to prepare myself before presenting my documents to the court."

Samuel thought a moment before replying.

"Yes, there is one. When you entered the city you had to pass through the old town outside the walls. Return there and ask directions for the Inn of Beshar; he is a thief but at least he is a cowardly one. He would think twice before robbing one with your scars of battle."

Casca thanked him for his hospitality and his advice. He rose from the cushions, smiling. "I hope to see you again, Samuel Ben Ezra."

The old man shook his head in the negative.

"I do not think that would be wise. My people are only barely tolerated here and if one such as yourself were seen here doing dealings with us it might lead to trouble. We Jews of the world must walk a careful line. I wish you good fortune but, please, do not come here again. It could lead to disaster for us both. I am too old to move and start again . . ."

He escorted Casca to the door, remaining carefully in the shadows, whispering.

"Remember what I have told you. Do not linger in this land or you will live to regret it, messenger or not. I can feel something that gives the aura of pain. Go home, Roman, while you still can."

Casca bid the old Jew farewell and made his way back outside the gates of the city. On his way, he bumped into a man whose face was hidden, knocking the smaller man to the ground. Reaching to help him up, his left hand grasped the sleeve of the other's robe, jostling the hood somewhat.

He quickly pulled the hood back into place, hiding his face in its shadows, and brushed off Casca's attempted apologies. He stopped in mid-speech when he saw the scar encircling Casca's wrist. Looking up at the scarred face of this foreigner, the man quickly slipped from Casca's grip and fled down the street without further word. He moved with a feeling of urgency, disappearing into the throng.

Casca shook his head, thinking that the man was sure a queer bird. No matter, he had to find shelter for the night. He went to reclaim his horse from the hostler and asked directions to the inn that Samuel had recommended.

The feeling of being watched stayed with him as he made his way to the inn. Twice he'd turned around quickly to see if he could catch the hidden eyes that were eerily scratching at the nape of his neck, but there was nothing.

He grumbled to himself. Maybe he was just tired and a little edgy. He knew for damned sure that he needed a drink, a bath, and a woman. Not necessarily in that order.

It didn't take him long to find the inn. It was located in what was left of the onetime great city of Asack, before Nev-Shapur had been built. Now, there were only a few buildings remaining to serve the caravans and itinerant travelers that arrived too late to find lodging inside the walls of Nev-Shapur.

The inn was typical—two stories of sunbaked brick with shuttered windows to let in the cool night air and a small fenced enclosure that served as a stable for the camels and horses of the travelers. After turning his horse over to a house slave, he entered the large main room and was greeted by the lumbering form of the master of the inn. Beshar, in his usual foul mood, advanced to meet the ragged man in his doorway. He had no time for tramps. His belly swayed with each heavy step, face shining from the rich food he consumed almost nonstop from rising to sleep.

He was stopped from ordering the stranger off his premises when the squarely-built figure in the doorway opened his palm and tossed Beshar three small silver coins of Chin. Beshar's hostile attitude made a complete turnaround to one of fawning subservience. For what the man had given was that which he loved most next to food, money. Casca had sized him up quickly; he had seen the type time and again. The only things that men like the innkeeper understood were money and fear.

Casca locked an eye on him and affected his sternest voice and manner.

"I have come a long way, landlord, and will have your best room and a bath readied for me. When I have cleansed myself and changed into more appropriate clothing, I will dine. Try to find something in this hovel that won't poison me."

Beshar fairly groveled. "Yes, lord, forgive me for not seeing instantly that you are a man of quality. But with the light behind you, your soiled clothes confused me for a moment. I can see clearly now that you are indeed a man of substance. Rest assured that I am honored that you would select my poor establishment for your stay." He snapped out an order and a serving wench came over. She was as thin as her master was obese. "Throw the man from the caravan out of his room and prepare for the foreign lord." The girl started to protest against evicting the current tenant, but was stopped by a quick backhand from Beshar. "Obey wench! If you like the camel herder that much, I'll see about having you travel with him when he heads to Bactria. Perhaps he could trade you to the Hephalites for a couple of good dogs."

The girl quailed at the thought of the Hephalites. The Persians called them the Huns. She left in a fearful rush to obey and send the caravan master on his way, regretting only that she would lose the two copper coins he had been giving her each night she slept with him. But nothing was worse than even the remote possibility of ending up in the felt yurts of the Hunnish tribes.

After sending the tavern wench off to do her duty, Beshar addressed himself again to the sunburned, travel-stained foreigner.

"Now, lord, will you take a seat while the room is being prepared? And perhaps some of the red wine of Shiraz would please you?"

Casca nodded in the affirmative. "Yea, and landlord, have my horse rubbed and curried and give him a full measure of grain. I want him to be presentable when I enter the city on the business of the Emperor of Chin." Casca knew that landlords were usually in the pay of whoever controlled the nearest city and that it wouldn't take long for word of his arrival to reach someone in authority. Settling his body on one of the wooden benches that served as seats for the plank tables, he put his pack beside him and adjusted his sword to a more comfortable position. Sighing deeply, he scratched a sore spot on his ass and grunted contentedly. It was good not to have to climb on the back of that four-legged torture chamber any more. After a bath and a shave he knew he would sleep deeply until cock's crow, and then . . . a new day, a new life for a while. The pouch of gems given him by Tzin would last a long time if he didn't do something stupid. He sipped the wine, enjoying the sharp, slightly resinous aftertaste, and was content to wait until his rooms were ready. It wouldn't be long, judging from the yelling going on upstairs as the camel driver was evicted.

A few more moments passed and the previous occupant of the room was going out the door, leaving behind a stream of oaths and curses that left Casca open-mouthed in admiration. He especially liked the one about, "May the sores from a thousand diseased camels infest the face of thy first born."

Wearily, he picked up his gear and climbed the stairs. It was a basic room with a clean bed and a jar for washing, also a strong bar to bolt the door from the inside. Well, if this was the best, he would hate to see the worst. But it would do for now.

In a ravine twenty-five miles from Nev-Shapur, a light flickered, glowing in the moonless night. The sound of chanting came, low and strange, from the entrance to the cave, the source of the light.

Inside were gathered a group of men. All kneeling, they prayed, their heads bowed. Hooded robes of rough, brown homespun wool covered their features, keeping their faces in constant shadow.

Torches danced in their iron bracks on the walls of the cavern, casting an eerie, quivering glow over the interior of the new refuge of the Brotherhood of The Lamb. The Elder stood before them, his face concealed in the folds of his hood. Only the members of the Inner Circle knew his true name. For the rest, it was enough that he was The Elder.

Behind him, illuminated by a row of bright burning torches, was the object of their adoration—"The Spear of Longinus," instrument of The Son of God's death.

The Elder raised his arm, showing delicate fingers without rings or other adornment. The Brotherhood was not given to opulent display of worldly goods. He spoke now, silencing the droning prayers of those on their knees. Though his body was slight in build and his robes seemingly too large for his frame, his voice rang out with the strength and authority of the righteous.

"Hear me, Brothers! The beast has returned from the lands beyond the wall. Praise be to The Lord, His Son, and to the thirteenth disciple, Izram, founder of our holy order. Some of you may have doubted that the beast truly lives. I say to you all now, he does live and he walks in the city of the idolator, Shapur. And, so that we may know him, as it is written in the 'Book of The Beast,' he wears the mark of punishment from the Elder Dacort. The scar on his right wrist, although the hand is whole again now, shows where Dacort had the beast's hand severed from his body. He has yet another visible scar on his face, brothers, and I swear to you, he does live yet and may God in his mercy curse his name for eternity."

There was an amen to this speech from the brethren on their knees, and he continued.

"Praise be to God, for the road that leads to His Son, Jesus, has returned and is again in our sight."

The Elder's voice rose, bouncing from the stone walls of the cavern that had served as their refuge since they'd been forced to flee the monastery in the desert due to the encroachment of barbarians and savage tribes of the heathenish Huns. Passion rode every word from the Elder's tongue, hatred and venom dripped from his mouth with every pronouncement. Pure, simple, burning hate beat at his followers. They wailed in anguish with their hatred of the animal, the spawn of evil, the beast that had driven his spear so cruelly into the side of their beloved and gentle Lamb on the Mount of Golgotha.

Then, as Dacort had done many years past, The Elder cried out for the heavens to hear them.

"Brothers, pray with me. Curse the name of Longinus, the 'Killer of God.' "

The brethren moaned and wailed, their souls filled with delicious ecstasy and pain. Sobbing out the hated name from their unseen mouths, their bodies twitching and twisted, they acted out the reliving of the scourging of Jesus. Whips and flails, mounted on their tips by balls of lead, were removed from beneath their robes and they began to beat themselves, the small lead balls striking into their flesh. They all cried out in glorious pain, *"Longinus, Longinus, Longinus!"*

The Elder's whipping words rose over the sounds of their anguish. "Remember the beast! He must not escape us again. He must be punished for all the days of his life. We, the true followers of Izram, are entrusted with the sacred duty of watching the beast and giving what pain we may to him when the opportunity arises. And, Brothers, the time will not be long in coming when we shall be able to give him all that he deserves. There is no punishment too great, no suffering possible that he does not deserve. As Izram has bade us to do in his teachings, we must hate... hate... hate. Until the day of the resurrection, when we shall at last be one in the spirit and glory of Jesus." As one, all responded with "Amen, Amen."

Like silent shadows, the members of the Brotherhood filtered out of the entrance to the cavern. It had been fortunate, they thought, that the beast had been found during the time that the Brotherhood gathered for their annual meeting. The word was taken back with them as they dispersed to their separate nations and cities, some going even to Rome or as far as the Isles of Brittania. All of the Brothers carried with them the identical message. "Casca lives, and is in Persia."

One of the members removed his rough garment of wool before climbing into his saddle, revealing below his own attire, richly flowing robes of state. He must hurry now back to his city of Nev-Shapur. It was he who had recognized the name of Casca Rufio Longinus when it had come to him from his spies in the city, and it was he who had brought the good news to the congregation of the Brotherhood. Now he must return in haste. There was much to do and prepare for before the sun rose tomorrow.

He found his reins and mounted. Striking the animal's flanks, he raced over the stones and sand of the plains and deserts, robes whipping in the wind, his horse lathering at the mouth, its heart straining with every stride. He cared not if the animal dies, as long as it got him back to Nev-Shapur before dawn. Rasheed, Vizier to Shapur II the King of Kings, was elated with his good fortune. He would find some way to punish the Roman. The time, as the Elder had said, was near. He was excited now, and determined to do even better than he had in the past, by taking some sort of direct action on his own that would bring his name to the attention of the Elder and enhance his stature in the Brotherhood.

He rode long that night, without stopping, and was successful in reaching the city wall before first light. His thin hawk-nosed face was familiar to the guards and they granted him immediate entrance through the gates reserved for the nobility and members of Shapur's royal court. Rasheed was the Vizier, advisor to Shapur, and the second most powerful man in the Empire.

His horse died of a ruptured heart before it could be led to the stables.

THREE

Casca slept until after cock's crow. Rested, he rose, washed, and finished dressing. Taking from his pack a robe of blue silk trimmed with gold thread, he placed it over a light shirt of chain mail. The robe reached to mid-thigh over the leather trousers he had traded for. They were soft and flexible, having been chewed to the suppleness of fine cloth by the teeth of the tribeswomen and then dyed a dark blue. He put a wide leather belt set with large brass rings around his waist and slung his sword from a leather halter, to hang by his right side in the Roman manner. His face was as tender as a baby's fanny after the scraping, cutting, and tugging required to get rid of the scruffy inch-long beard that had sprouted on his face. Fanning his hand over his jaw, he winced at the memory of the barber they had sent him. The man could have qualified for a position as a torturer with any of the better dungeons and slave camps.

Finally satisfied with his appearance, he went down the rickety wooden stairs to the main room. His new appearance of wealth, as represented by the robes of silk, properly awed his obese host.

Beshar fawned over his new guest and tried to get him to eat at his establishment, but after testing the menu from the previous night, Casca decided to pass and try to get something better inside the city of Nev-Shapur. He knew it would be long before the local authorities rounded him up. He was thankful that he had the letters from Tzin in his pouch and his own decree of nobility. Those should serve to give him a good welcome. From what he had heard, those from Rome were less than welcome in the lands of the Sassanids and he had a long way to go before reaching the Mediterranean. It would be best if he could do that as a free man and not as a slave.

He didn't figure there would be too many problems finding someone to translate the letters he carried, for Nev-Shapur sat directly on the silk road, and on his way he had seen many caravans with merchants from Chin carrying goods to the west. He wished he had been able to learn to decipher the wriggling block script that served as writing for the people of Chin, but it had been too much for him to figure out. He felt lucky to have even a knack for spoken languages. Stepping out into the full light of day, he entered into a throng of people lined up to enter the gates of the city. There were merchants, farmers, tourists and pilgrims, and women carrying vases and packs on their heads who walked with long, graceful steps. The clothing styles were as varied as the people. Nomads from the steppes in their leather trousers blended among those in the almost universal peasant dress of a simple gray or brown homespun waist-length shirt, tied with a rope or piece of cloth about the waist.

Perfumed ladies, with elaborate headdresses and silken wear, reclined in their slave-borne litters beside the women of the fields. All waited quietly in line for their turn to be admitted through the walls of the city. There was no disorder or shoving, each awaited his turn, for such was the word of the King. The nobles of higher rank entered through one of the gates reserved for personages of noble lineage, but all others entered there passing through the inspection of the household guards, brilliantly dressed and armored warriors in the purple tunics of Persia that covered a scaled *jazerant* of armor, rippling in the morning sun like the scales of a carp.

Horses and pack animals were not permitted within the city walls. Only the warriors of the King rode through the streets; the rich and noble were carried on litters. Wheelbarrows and carts, pulled or pushed by human muscle, took care of such items as needed to be brought inside. The King disliked the odor of animal waste on the streets and it was also unsightly, therefore it was forbidden. When it was Casca's turn to pass before the inspection of the gate guards, he held out his packet of papers from the Son of Heaven Beyond the Wall That Runs Forever. The Guards inspected the sealed packet closely and questioned him as to its contents. Casca explained that it came from the Emperor of Chin to the King of the Persians and that he was its courier and a noble.

The guards conferred among themselves for a few moments and then took Casca inside a small room that served as a resting place for the different guard shifts. Inside he was told to wait. Their attitude was formal and correct. There was no sign of discourtesy, and if they were curious about why a man with blue eyes would be carrying a message from Chin, they didn't show it. He was told that he would be taken care of soon and was left alone under the watchful eye of one guard who had the look of Arabistan about him. Dark, piercing eyes over a hooked nose and thin lips were set in a face that was all angles, as weathered dark as aged leather. Casca had to cool his heels for about an hour before a court official showed up with his packet of papers in hand. Following him was a middle-aged Oriental who questioned Casca about his mission to the court. It satisfied the official's inquiry as to the validity of Casca's papers when Casca showed him his seal of office, the Chu Hou Wang of the Baron of Khitai, as ordained by the Son of Heaven, the Emperor Tzin. The official told him he would be given an audience with the King on the following day. Until that time he would be moved from his quarters at the inn and shown to facilities set aside for such purposes. When Casca asked about returning to get his gear and horse he was told that all things would be taken care of for him. He was to come now. Casca was smart enough not to argue, even though his stomach was starting to growl. He hadn't had a chance to get anything to eat, but maybe he could get something wherever they were taking him. Leaving the guards' shack, he found a military escort was waiting for him, and to his surprise, there was a slave-borne litter in which he was to be carried to whatever destination his host had in mind.

"Why not? Might as well enjoy it." He settled

himself in on soft padded cushions and drew the curtains partially closed to keep out the bright sun. The slaves raised the litter off the cobblestoned street smoothly, with no jerking, and the escort formed up on both sides with a mounted horseman in front to break trail through the swarms of people crowding the morning streets. Casca reclined on one elbow and watched the passersby between the curtains. At least he was off to an auspicious beginning. At the horseman's command the streets emptied to either side of the litter and its escort, leaving a clear path for them to travel. This was a city that obeyed without hesitation. In due course, after many turnings and twistings, he and his bodyguard came to the inner city where the King and his court resided in opulent Oriental splendor reminiscent of Xerxes the Great. Tall columns and walls decorated with glazed bricks depicting hunting scenes and mythical animals brightened up the way. Once inside the walls of the inner city, the hubbub of the outside was effectively cut off and only came through as a distant murmuring. A light thump and the litter was set down. With some regret, Casca eased himself from his transport, and made a note to buy one for himself one day.

The Persian court official who had come for him showed him into a hallway lined with tall pillars of carved stone that held a massive roof painted with the glories of Persia's past. The Persians loved color almost as much as did the nobles of the court of Chin. Only the Romans seemed to have an affection for sterile cold edifices. He supposed that it gave them the illusion of being firm and righteous, not giving in to frills. Passing numbers of the beautifully armored Warriors of Shapur, he admired the discipline in them; there was no sign of ass-grabbing at all. These were professionals who took pride in their profession. In short time he was completely lost in the maze of halls and passages that they passed through until they came at last to a halt. Casca's escort opened a door admitting him to a large, comfortable room with a sleeping cot made soft with down-stuffed cushions of red. On a table food waited; obviously his arrival had been anticipated. His host bade him take his ease, that he would be sent for in due time. The letters from Tzin were not returned. His host explained that a formal translation would have to be made of them and a copy entered in to the court records, at which time the King would look them over before deciding to receive the emissary from Chin. Before leaving, Casca was requested to surrender his sword, though allowed to keep his knife. He was told that there was nothing personal in the disarming of him, it was just policy and his weapons would be returned afterwards. Backing his way out, Casca was left to attack with eagerness the rack of lamb cooked in mint and sage. There was nothing he could do now but wait for the King to send for him and who the hell could tell how long that would take. Kings moved in their own peculiar timeframes and the urgencies of lesser beings were seldom worthy of any consideration.

But then, kings, priests, and whores all wanted to do everything their own way. Kings, because no one else was really important to them; priests, because they wanted you to think they were important; and whores, because time was money. Casca appreciated the whores' reasons more than the others.

After about an hour, the door to his chambers opened and a slave girl entered to take out the dirty dishes. Not a bad-looking piece. He eyed her up and down; she smiled back shyly at the scar-faced, blue-eyed barbarian who was leering at her with such obvious interest. As his eyes moved down to her thinly covered breasts, she could feel the nipples harden. A little reluctantly she left with her dishes and wondered if the stranger would send for her this night. As she went out of the door Casca noted that two sentries had been assigned to his room, one on each side, and from the looks on their faces neither one had much of a sense of humor. Well, he knew the type. There would be no use in trying to get any information out of them. Their minds were so locked up with being what they thought was the epitome of the good soldier that they probably went to the crapper by the numbers.

He spent three days in his chamber with his meals being brought in by the same girl. He did manage once to talk her into a quickie, which, though fast, was still quite satisfying. The rest of his possessions had been brought to him the day after he had been taken to the palace. Since that time he had not been permitted to leave his rooms or even go out into the hallway. So like all men in forced isolation, he did the only thing one can do—he slept, waking for a time to eat and stretch, then, after a few hours, dozing off again. Anything to help use up the hours until he would be sent for.

On the morning of the fourth day an official,

wearing a high-ridged plumed helmet of steel overlaid with bronze, came for him. The two sentries formed up, one on either side, with the officer leading. He was again taken through a labyrinth of hallways and corridors until he was admitted to an antechamber where a number of other visitors, diplomats, and emissaries were lined up, giving their names and their business to the court scribe who interviewed them. Casca waited his turn in line behind a Median governor who was trying to get a government subsidy to build some new public office buildings.

Casca wore the best of his two silk robes he'd brought with him. He knew that they would give him some stature in the eyes of the court officials; they were worth their weight in gold. When his turn came he stated his business as being ordered by the Son of Heaven, the Emperor Tzin, to deliver his message of good will and affection to His Royal Highness, the King of Kings of Persia, Shapur II. Also, to advise his royal cousin of the new threat developing from the savage tribes who inhabited the great wastelands of the steppes. The Huns were on the move again. Casca made sure the scribe included in his notes that he was a noble of the court of the Peacock Throne.

After he and the others had waited for some time they were finally led through one last corridor of the massive carved stones that reached ten times the height of a tall man, passing even more of the palace guards until they were finally admitted to the presence. The Magnificent Hall of the King of Kings outshone anything Imperial Rome had ever conceived and was only second to the Court of the

Imperial City at Chang-an. Massive carved bas-reliefs of winged bulls combined with vividly painted frescoes of kings hunting lions from chariots. Others depicted the kings of Persia and their conquests over the barbarian tribes. One showed the Emperor Valerian being forced to kneel, head bowed before his captor, Shapur I, *Shahan shah Eran ut an Eran,* King of Kings of Persia and non-Persia, one of the greatest of the line of Aryan kings.

In the hall, a thousand nobles lay prostrate on their faces before the throne; Casca and the new supplicants were made to do likewise. The feel of the stone floors was cool to his chin. Bronzed braziers gave off aromatic wisps of incense to be whisked away by the black slaves fanning the royal person, while his Vizier performed the ritual to open this day's hearings. In a high nasal voice, Rasheed cried out the glories of his master and called down from the sky the blessings of *Ahuramazda* upon this proceeding and all those herein. Shapur II waved his hand and permitted those prostrate before him to rise and set eyes upon him.

Shapur sat upon a throne of alabaster; on either side the winged bulls of Assyria guarded the royal person from evil spirits. Casca whistled under his breath—Shapur was one hell of a man by anyone's standards. Instead of a staff of office, he held a sword whose point rested between his gold-sandaled feet. His sword arm was bare and Casca had the feeling that it wasn't too unusual for the King to administer justice himself, as he kept his sword clear from the robes that covered him to the knees. His robes were of woven silver thread and purple silk, fringed with tassels of braided gold. His legs were bare except for a set of boots similar to the Roman *caligulae*. Both arms and legs were strong and knotted with muscle. The face of Shapur rested not under a crown, but under a warrior's Helm of Iron, set about with silver bands. A nasal guard raised to rest on the crest of the helmet.

Shapur's face was dark from years of campaigning; lean, with the muscles in his jaws constantly working; a thin, yet sensuous mouth with no humor in the lips. He watched everything and everyone with the gaze of a predatory bird. Unblinking, pitch-black eyes missed nothing. When he spoke his voice was not loud, but every word could be clearly heard to the farthest extremities of his court. It was the voice of one born to lead, the voice of Shapur II, King of Kings, and you could bet your ass no one who ever saw him would argue about it.

Casca stood silently as one petitioner after another was led before the King, his case to be disposed of in short order. Casca quickly learned the King had no time for the long flowery greetings and blessings so common in the Chinese court. When the petitioner started to drone he was quickly cut short and made to move on to his case without any hesitations. Shapur gave his judgments in the same voice, and each man who stood before him could not help glancing repeatedly at the bared sword in his master's hand. Several were sentenced to death for one offense or another. These thanked their lord for his kindness and went off to an appointment with the headsman's ax.

One who had stolen from the taxes was given an

unusual sentence. Shapur, eyes piercing through to the soul of the thieving tax official, spoke softly. "You, who I have trusted, love gold more than me. When you came to me and asked for my favor your words were like gold and that shall be your punishment." The thief was led off, sobbing, to the torture chambers, where the royal inquisitors melted down ingots of pure gold, forced open the man's mouth, and filled it with the molten metal. . . .

Casca waited beneath the bas-relief friezes depicting the glories of the Persian kings, listening carefully to the dialogue taking place between the hawk-nosed ruler and a thin, mild-mannered man from the Nile.

Imhept stood, head bowed before the King of Kings. He wore his thin robes of linen with an unmistakable dignity that seemed out of place in one so slight and mild in manner. Imhept's eyes were deep brown and behind them lay a sparkle that belied his advanced years. Shapur's Vizier had sent for him to come to Nev-Shapur to advise them on the construction of new edifices and also to aid them in their new program of expanding the networks of irrigation systems that had fallen into disrepair.

Shapur was somewhat puzzled by the Egyptian. He was used to overawing everyone about him, not only by the virtue of his throne, but also by his own strong personality. He was not just a king, but a warrior to be reckoned with.

But this calm, elderly man with his shaved head showed no sign of fear or apprehension. Shapur had known few that had not feared him and they were either mad or one of the holy hermits who lived in the trackless wastes of the desert. This man, like the holy ones, was at peace with himself. Shapur knew that here was one who would speak the truth, though it may cost him his head. And that was a man to be valued or destroyed—there was no middle ground for such as the Egyptian standing before him.

Shapur stroked his square-cut beard with long, graceful fingers. "Egyptian, it is told me by my Vizier that you are a man of great learning and wisdom who has devoted his life to study. Now I would pose a question for you."

Imhept raised his face to look in the eyes of Shapur. "I will answer if able, Lord."

Shapur pursed his lips, thoughtful for a moment, phrasing the question properly in his mind before speaking. "Scholar, the question is this: Of all the achievements of mankind throughout the ages, from all the known races and lands, what has been the single most significant achievement of man since his beginnings?"

Imhept closed his eyes and nodded slowly—once, twice—then opened his dark eyes and smiled as a teacher would to a beloved but wayward child. Shapur shifted uneasily on his throne. A small smile played around the lips of Imhept. "Lord of Hosts, King of Kings. The single greatest achievement of man, that has permitted all else to come forth is—the plow."

Shapur shook his head as if throwing off a bothersome thought. "Do not take liberties with me, scholar."

Imhept bowed his head again. "I do not say this in jest, Lord."

Shapur was still confused. "The plow? But what of the great pyramids and temples of your own land? What of the libraries where the knowledge of man is accumulated that others may learn from the past? What of the great kings who brought prosperity and glory to their nations? Do you say these are of less importance than the common plow that peasants use to till their fields?"

Imhept nodded. "As you have said, Lord, so it is. One must not start at the end of a thought but at the beginning. All that you have said would not have come to pass without the lowly plow to till the fields. For with the plow man began to grow. With the plow man was able to plant more than he could eat and the threat of starvation was removed for the most part. This gave man time to organize, to build cities over which kings could rule. For with cities there had to come law and order.

"And from the plow came many of the other achievements of man. For example, if there is a surplus of grain to be stored, then there is need for containers to store it in—hence pottery. From storage there had to come a means to count and determine how much would be needed to last a village until the next season and how much would be available for trade. Hence, mathematics were needed. And writing, so that one could keep track of what went where and what agreements were reached between buyer and seller. This is naturally a simplification, as the actual total of arts and sciences that came from the plow would take days to enumerate. But suffice to say that the leisure time the plow afforded man gave rise to those sciences and arts by which the great temples and structures were built. For the early village beginnings, where leaders were needed to rule, did give rise to the great houses and empires. Lord, all this would not be if the ordinary plow had not been."

Shapur was impressed. The logic behind the thought progression was clear, the extrapolation easy to follow. The very simplicity of the idea made it complicated. Shapur was satisfied with the answer.

"Scholar you have pleased us. It is by my command that you are made advisor to the court and given jurisdiction over the fields and waters of my lands. I will call on you from time to time. Do as you have done now and always speak the truth and you will find your rewards will be great." He regretted instantly the automatic promise of reward and the next statement would have been the threat of punishment for failure or lying. He knew that neither would have any effect on the Egyptian. He was what he was, a man committed to the truth and to learning. He could not be induced to be other than that.

"You may go scholar. Travel where you will and return to me in three months, and tell of what you have seen and what needs to be done to the plains and sands so that Persia may bear fruit again, as it did when Cyrus the Acmeanid ruled. The land has been too long barren. Go and help bring back the fields and orchards." The Egyptian was dismissed and left the hall. Casca watched the thin figure leave and wondered at the minds of men who saw things so clearly without emotion or pride.

It was his turn. The Vizier, reading from a scroll,

called out his name and motioned for him to step forth in front of the throne and kneel. While on his knees, the Vizier read off his titles and honors accorded him by the Emperor of Chin.

Shapur snapped his fingers and motioned for Casca to rise. Casca stood at attention as Shapur looked him over. He felt as if the Persian king was eating into his soul with his dark eyes, and he knew something of what the thief had felt. This man would order you sliced into pieces without a second's hesitation.

Shapur spoke. "You are Casca Longinus, Baron of Khitai and warlord to the Emperor of Chin." A statement, not a question. "It is strange that one from Rome would have such honors. I welcome the Emperor's words and the warning about the resurgence of the Hephalites. We will tend to them. But what of you, Roman?" The last word was spoken bitterly.

Casca knew he was walking on thin ice and picked his words carefully. "I am what the missive from the Peacock Throne says. A man who has served his master well with loyalty and the sword."

Shapur grinned thinly. "And what of Rome? Is not your first allegiance to the Caesars?"

Casca shook his head. "My first loyalty, Lord, is to those that show the same to me. True, I have served in the legions of Rome but have been ill-rewarded for it." With that he pulled his silk robes down over his shoulders and bared his back to the King.

Shapur wet his lips at the sight of the crisscrossing of scars on the muscled back, mixed with deep cuts from edged weapons. Casca turned back around to face the King. "Those, and my years on the slave bench of war galleys, have paid off any debt I have to Imperial Rome. I am my own man."

Shapur liked the scar-faced man's answers. That he was a warrior was obvious and as one fighting man to another, Shapur had to respect him. "Where would you go from here, Casca, Baron of Khitai?"

Casca shrugged. "I but follow the threads of my fate, Lord."

Shapur thought for a moment. "I would speak further with you. As a warlord it might prove of interest to learn how the warriors of Chin conduct their battles. You will dine with me this evening."

Casca was dismissed. Bowing, he backed away from the imperial presence and was taken back to his quarters, a feeling of relief surging over him. He knew that it had been close and perhaps wasn't over with yet. He would find out his fate tonight.

An hour after the sun had set, he was sent for and escorted once more through the winding labyrinth, then up several flights of stairs and finally out onto an open courtyard, set three stories above the main floor. Shapur waited in loose robes of cool linen. Full-grown palm trees and other flowers and plants Casca couldn't name decorated the rooftop garden. He understood why the King preferred the rooftop garden to take his evening meal —the evening breeze cooled the air. Guards remained unobtrusive at their posts, just out of earshot. Slave girls came and went, setting the low table with sweetmeats and delicacies. Shapur motioned for Casca to join him on the couch opposite the table. Torches and lamps lit the scene and

Shapur was at ease. "Sit down, warrior, and we'll talk of the things men do."

Casca obeyed and reclined on the couch. Shapur motioned toward the food. "Help yourself, Roman."

Casca tried a couple of jellied plover's eggs, washing them down with a wine he hadn't tasted before, smacking his lips over the taste. "Good, damned good." Tearing off a piece of roasted antelope, he sunk his teeth into the meat and chewed slowly as Shapur looked on and ate nothing.

Shapur watched his guest eat, noting through veiled eyes, every detail about the man before him —the way he moved, the thick cords in his wrists, the scars. How could he use this man who came from behind the Wall of Chin? For him to carry letters stating he was a noble of the court and a warlord of the Hosts meant he had value. True, he was of Roman origins, but Shapur would not deny himself the usage of capable men. If the Roman became troublesome, he could always be easily removed. Shapur rinsed his mouth with a sip of spring water. Patiently, he waited until his guest had finished his meal.

"Tell me of the land behind the Wall. Take your time, we have all this night. Tell me of the land, the kings, the women, and especially of their methods of warfare." He noticed a slight movement on Casca's part when he mentioned speaking of the Chinese way of war. Good. The man was reluctant to give away information concerning those to whom he had given his loyalties.

Shapur eased Casca's mind. "I have no designs on Chin. It is enough that I can control my own lands and keep the barbarians at bay. If ever I turned my armies to the East, how long do you think it would be before I had another Roman invasion force coming at me from the rear? Only a fool fights on more than one front."

Casca understood what the King meant and began to talk, telling him of the Court of Ch'ang, of the cities and rivers, of lands reaching so far that a man could not ride across them in a year, of high mountains and deep valleys. And he spoke of the thinking process of the Chinese and of their tacticians. One in particular was named Sung Tzu. Casca regretted again his inability to read the ideograms of the Chinese, for he would have liked to have brought with him a copy of Sung Tzu's writings, the *Art of War*. He had had the book read to him by slaves and friends and much of it he remembered, but not all. The Chinese were the world's best record-keepers and he had also heard of other stratagems that showed how the Chinese loved to use the oblique approach to battle and delighted in outwitting their opponents more than they did in killing them. Shapur was also interested in the Huns, so Casca related a tale about how a Chinese general used three thousand condemned men to defeat a Hunnish army of fifty thousand.

Shapur, for the first time, broke into a short laugh of appreciation at the tale. His dark eyes sparkled with the closest thing he had to a sense of humor. "Lord Casca, I have been most pleased by you and your stories this evening. I would make a bargain with you. Are you interested?"

Casca said that he was. There was power about Shapur and his curiosity about the man made him reluctant to leave Persia.

Shapur nodded. "Good. This is what I would

have. Stay in my court and render me the same service you did to the land of Chin. We have many of the same enemies. I would put your mind at ease where Rome is concerned. In the event of another war with Rome, I will release you from your oath so that you may not be divided in your loyalties. I know you say that you have no great love for the Caesars, but it is still best if I relieve you from ever having to make a choice between us. It is true that a child may speak harshly of his parents and even rebel against them, but the child will, even if he feels he has been badly abused by the parents, more often than not, come to their aid when danger threatens. And you are still a child of Rome."

Casca was dismissed, leaving Shapur to watch the dawn rise over the flat roofs of his city. Casca knew that before he left the rooftop, Shapur's mind had already left him far behind and was now on some other matter.

But Shapur had by no means forgotten what he had spoken to Casca about. The next afternoon a messenger delivered a scroll carrying Casca's commission in the royal forces and assigning him to the Household Guard with the rank of regimental commander. He was moved forthwith into new quarters. It was a small house, sparsely furnished, but already staffed with four slaves, consisting of a cook, a personal body slave, and one who was to advise him on the customs of the land and to oversee the household. The last was a soldier from the armies of Shapur who had been given a reprieve from death in order that he might familiarize Casca with the order of battle of the Persian forces. He was given no immediate duties, other than to keep in readiness for whatever his new master might require of him.

Shapur was a solitary man given to spending long hours alone. Even his favorite concubines knew not to disturb him when he was in his thoughts. Most of these had to do with retrieving the lands still in the hands of Romans or any others that he felt were his. He knew in time he would move to the west after he had secured his borders to the east and north. Then he would be free to mount a major campaign against Rome and regain the lands granted Rome by the treaty of Narses. Shapur would never forgive his grandfather for giving in. True, Narses had suffered a severe reverse when he had lost a major campaign in Armenia, in which the Romans captured not only his treasury but also his harem. Narses had ceded to the Romans, Armenia and the steppes of Mesopotamia with the hill country, and Singagara, on the west side of the Tigris and reaching as far as Gordyene. In exchange for this outrageous payoff the Romans returned his household to Narses.

If Shapur had been in the same situation, there would have been no doubt in his mind that he himself would have slit the throats of his children and wives before surrendering one yard of land to anyone.

Shapur grinned bleakly at the rememberance of how he came to the throne after the death of Ormized II, the son of Narses. A rebellious clique had put all the sons of Narses to death with exception of Ormized, who escaped to the Romans. They'd used him as pretender to the throne for their own purpose, to counter this threat from what many of their people would consider the legitimate successor to the throne, and used him as a rallying point for rebellion. The clique brought to the throne Shapur II, himself a son of Ormized, but born after his father's death.

In Shapur, they thought they had a perfect figurehead. The young man would be easy enough to control. But Shapur was cut from stronger cloth than his so-called advisors would have thought. At fourteen, he organized among young men of the nobility a secret guard sworn to him alone. One by one, these young nobles came into positions of power inside the infra structure of the palace and when the time was right—and Shapur not yet seventeen—they struck. All that long night riders went forth carrying the sword and torch. Each of the young men had recruited five others who, in their turn, did the same until there were over five thousand young warriors, the oldest of whom had not reached twenty.

These young lions removed for all times any threat to the throne of Shapur II. He himself took the heads of the Vizier and his sons, then personally supervised the torture of all surviving prisoners. In an act of piety he permitted them to die by the light of *Ahura-mazda*. He staked them out in the courtyard, forced water down their throats to prolong the agony, and let them bake in the sun until their flesh cracked open. The sun blinded them (he had also cut their eyelids off so they could look directly into the glory of God). Shapur was king and none who contested his will would be permitted to live, not anyone, not his wives or even the flesh of his flesh. A king cannot rule by compassion where power is concerned. Power is the only reason for living—to be weak is to give up that reason. And one could always sire more children.

Casca was taken by members of the household guard to the armory, where he was fitted for his armor of gilded iron scales. The rippling metal resembled the scales of the golden carp. The helmet was likewise decorated with a steel mesh neck guard; the helmet was of one piece, basically no more than a round conical cap with ear flaps of steel that could be tied under the chin. A cloth of green silk was wrapped around the brim of the cap to show his rank in the Guard. The armorers, and others present, gave him questioning, slightly hostile looks, as if his fair hair and light-colored eyes didn't belong. With the casting out of the Greek Parthians, those with his features were not readily welcomed in the armies of the new empire. But they also knew better than to question one that had obviously been favored by the King.

For Casca's part, he didn't give a rat's ass if they liked it or not. He had more on his mind. On his way over from his quarters he had run into the Vizier, Rasheed. The way the sneaky-looking little bastard smiled and bowed to him gave him shivers up his spine. He had been around long enough to know that the kind of look he had been given didn't mean anything good for him. But what had he done to earn the Vizier's enmity? Well, as the saying went, time would tell. For now, he just wanted to know what Shapur had up his sleeve.

It was three weeks before Shapur summoned him to his presence again. This time they were to meet on the city parade field where Casca had been told a small ceremony was to take place to finalize his acceptance into the ranks. As ordered, Casca appeared in his new armor and was given a bay mare to ride to the grounds, escorted by twenty of the King's own personal guards.

Once on the parade grounds, Casca saw the field was lined with mounted troops, all fully armed, lance heads held erect. There were two ranks facing each other. In the center was a burning pyre, about which were gathered what were obviously priests and nobles of the court.

Casca went to face whatever it was they had in mind for him. He didn't think they were going to jail or try and kill him; there would have been no need to go through this much trouble. His escort guided him to a pavilion of multicolored fabrics where Shapur waited. Once there, he was permitted to dismount and kneel before the King. Shapur rose from his field chair and stood before him, dressed in plain soldier's armor.

"Casca Longinus, my Vizier has made a request that before you are permitted to command troops of the Empire it would be well if you would now reject the gods of Rome and all others, including the gods of those who follow the Christus. For in my lands, the supreme deity is the Sun in the manifestation of *Ahura-mazda*. All others are lesser entities and only *Ahura-mazda* is supreme. Will you reject all worship of any other gods and put none else before the holy light of Sun?"

Casca thought to himself, this is really dumb,

but if that's what he wants, why not? Raising his face, he vowed, "I will, and gladly, my King, for as you know the gods of Rome have served me ill." Rasheed stood to the King's left, wearing ceremonial robes of deep green decorated with gold emblems of the sun set in geometric patterns, smiling as he had before. Casca wondered what the sour-faced wretch found so damned amusing about the proceedings. After acknowledging his willingness to do sacrifice to the Sun, Casca was led by two Magi to the burning pyre.

It was large enough to set two full grown steers inside it to be roasted. Following the wisemen's lead, he bowed three times as he approached and then knelt before the altar. A lamb had its throat cut and was given to him. This, Casca consigned to the flames, thankful it wasn't something worse. The despised Phoenicians, worshippers of Baal, gave their first born child to the flames to prove their loyalties. The lamb was accepted by the flames, as if it had any choice. Omens were read and forecasts given. All was expected to be favorable and Casca was given leave to rise.

Shapur came to him and embraced him before the mounted troops. Casca felt again a twinge of uneasiness. He liked, but also feared Shapur. The man was strong and wore the mantle of power about him easily. But Casca hadn't expected this aspect of the King, that he was also a religious fanatic. That could prove dangerous. For when anyone was too involved with gods, it spelled trouble for everyone else around him. No matter how smart the King might be, the gods would always have the last laugh.

Shapur escorted Casca back to his mount. "I am pleased that you have not been reluctant to give your oath, for I have need of you now and in the next week you will be given your first assignment. I will send for you. Go now."

Dismissed, Casca was relieved that the ceremony was all there was to the day's proceedings, and as he rode off wondered what plans the king now had for him. The Vizier smiled and bowed to him in a most friendly manner. For some reason this disturbed Casca.

Casca spent the next days keeping pretty much to himself, avoiding the desire to visit some of the gambling and wenching houses of which the city of Nev-Shapur had an abundance. He still felt uneasy and decided that it would be better to keep away from anything that might possibly give an enemy anything to use against him.

FOUR

Another two weeks passed with Casca remaining in his self-enforced confinement. True, he had sent out from time to time for one or another of the famous Persian courtesans to visit him in his room —sloe-eyed, dusky, warm-blooded women who'd learned the art of pleasing men when they were still children. After all, he still had normal needs and they'd served to keep the edge off his temper.

He received notice of his departure in the form of a letter delivered by one of Shapur's guards, a member of the Immortals. Casca was not of this elite unit. Only those with pure Persian bloodlines, from noble families, were permitted to serve in their ranks. Even the messenger, who held the lowest rank in the Guards, was of an ancient and noble house that traced its lineage back over three hundred years. At Shapur's command any of these people would, without hesitation, drive their daggers into their hearts or into one of their own blood.

The Immortals were chosen as children and taken from their families when no older than ten. From that time on they were trained for one thing only, this being absolute obedience to the King of Kings.

The letter informed Casca to prepare himself to leave in two days and that before his departure he was to come to Shapur for a final premission briefing in which the operation would be explained.

As ordered, Casca presented himself to the majordomo and was ushered without ceremony into Shapur's private quarters. Bowing low, Casca waited for permission to stand erect. Permission was soon given with an offhanded wave of Shapur's strong fingers.

"Well, Casca, are you ready for your first assignment?" There could be but one response to the question, yet it was still with a sense of uneasiness that Casca answered.

"Of course, Lord. I await your command." He slapped his sword hand to his breast in salute. Shapur nodded, playing at his beard with his fingers as was the habit of the Persian when deep in thought. A thin smile played at the corner of Shapur's eyes.

"When last we talked you told of a ruse used by a Chinese general a century or two ago while engaged in battle with the Hephalites. The memories of those savages are not long and I would see if the same plan could be used again."

Casca swallowed. "You mean the three thousand who . . . ?"

"Exactly!" Shapur smiled openly, showing strong white teeth. "When you return to your residence an escort will be waiting for you. He shall take you to join your army, which I dispatched a month ago to the frontiers of Sogdiana to serve as bait. From intelligence reports we know that the Hephalites are on the move to join us in battle. They know that if they can eliminate my army there it will free the entire countryside for their looting and pillaging for some weeks' time. But if you succeed and destroy them that will secure my frontiers in the north and east for at least a couple of years. I could then turn my attention to other pressing matters without being bothered excessively by large raiding parties."

Shapur paused for a moment, his eyes reflecting honesty.

"Serve me well in this matter, Casca, and you shall find that I know how to reward as well as to punish."

Shapur motioned with his hand down, shoving the fingers forward toward the exit. "You may leave!"

Casca bowed his way out of the royal chambers and returned to his dwelling to find that his gear had already been packed by the escort, his servants dismissed, and the house closed. All that he would require on his journey was methodically placed in packs on the back of the horses.

Casca grumbled to himself. "Shapur doesn't let any grass grow under the feet of anyone who works for him, that's for damned sure."

His escort was composed of ten men from a light cavalry detachment, expert archers all of them. During the journey they rode like the demons of Shaitan were on their tails, stopping only once each night for an hour's rest, changing mounts in relays six or seven times a day. By utilizing these means they'd covered over one hundred miles per day and on the evening of the third day had arrived at the valley of Bazhari, where his Persian host awaited Casca's arrival. They had not arrived too soon as far as he was concerned.

Passing sentries and checkpoints of security, they were admitted into the main camp, where Casca was guided to a large pavilion that was to serve as his headquarters. Word of his arrival had already reached his regimental commanders and they stood in two ranks, one to either side of the tent, at rigid attention.

Casca entered, stomping the dust from his boots and pounding his chest to rid it of the day's dirt. Sand clouds flew from him at every thump of his fist. He eyed the commanders. All had the look of tough men. Only two were under thirty years of age and even they had visible scars to show they were not novices to battle. But Casca could see in their eyes the retention of doubt about this foreigner who'd come to command them. That they would obey him, he had no doubt; Shapur's discipline was much too rigidly enforced for them to consider doing otherwise. Yes, they would obey. But they wouldn't like it worth a damn.

A field desk and chair were in position at the rear of the tent. Casca marched straight to them and seated himself after acknowledging the reluctant bowing of his subordinate commanders. Pouring a drink of water from a carafe, he washed the dust of the trail from his throat before speaking.

"Which one of you is the superior officer?"

A Persian with a slight Greek cast to his features stepped forward and bowed, his scaled armor rippling in the light of the oil lamps. His helmet was tucked under one arm, his hand to the hilt of a long straight sword. The gray in his hair and his hard dark eyes were enough to gain him notice in a grouping of soldiers.

"I am Indemeer, Commander of the *Cataphracti*." Casca was familiar with this unit—Heavy Cavalry, whose horses as well as their riders were covered with heavy armor. The charge of the *Cataphracti* was hard to resist. The lances they used in battle were so heavy that the riders tied a rope near the center of it, attaching the other end to the necks of their steeds. Utilizing the strength of the animal to bear the weight of the lance, they would tuck the butt of the weapon into a leather socket at their hip, guiding the point of the lance with one hand while guilding the horse's movements with the other. Their helmets were of one piece that reached below the chin with only slits for eye-holes in them. They were a fearsome offensive force when used properly, and next to the Immortals, the most favored of the Persian Hosts.

Casca acknowledged the ranking commander. "Welcome, Indemeer. I trust you're ready to give me a situation report?"

Indemeer nodded confidently. "But of course, Commander." Casca took another drink of water. "Then proceed! The rest of you be at ease and make yourself comfortable. If any of you have individual information to report, wait until after the general briefing, then we'll get down to any specifics pertaining to your troops." He indicated for Indemeer to begin his report.

The Persian snapped his fingers and one of his junior officers came forth, handing the old warrior two scrolls. He unrolled them and placed them side by side on the field table, pointing to the one facing Casca's left. It was, as Casca could readily see, a map of the immediate region. On it Indemeer had lined the disposition of the Persian forces in red and the Huns in black. Speaking softly, but with tones that came from years of command and self-assurance, Indemeer began his report.

"The savages are approaching from the north and east at a good rate of march. We have scouts out keeping up with them and each day their reports are sent to us in relays so that by now we should have their movements reported twice a day. At their current rate of march they should reach this point in two days' time." Indemeer indicated a large plain in the form of a valley. Casca stopped him with a nod of his head.

"Is the valley you're pointing at the one we're in now?"

Indemeer shook his head. "No! That one is one day's march from our present location."

Casca told him to continue.

"The savages number sixty thousand, who, as I am sure you know, are all mounted horsemen, each one of them an archer and most carrying light lances for close combat."

Casca responded to the light sarcasm in Indemeer's voice. "Yes, I know the Huns well and have probably had as much experience with them as anyone here. Now, get on to something I don't know!"

Indemeer accepted the rebuke. He'd just been testing to see if this stranger was able to handle command and assert the authority designated to him by Shapur. Before he could continue Casca asked him for the disposition and numbers of their own forces. Indemeer indicated the red lines depicting each of the encampments around them.

"We have twenty thousand warriors, of which five thousand are my own Heavy Chargers by order of the King, as sign of his favor." Again the touch of sarcasm, Casca choosing this time to ignore it. Indemeer continued. "The balance of our forces are comprised of ten thousand light cavalry, all expert archers, and five thousand infantry."

Casca scanned the map carefully, noting the terrain differences. "Have you thought of a place to engage the Huns?"

The officer pointed to a plain outside the valley two days distant. "Here is where we will meet the enemy, with the valley to our backs. We shall place our infantry in the center at the entrance to the valley and position our cavalry on each flank inside. When the Huns charge, our center will fall back, luring them inside, at which point our two strong flanks will charge down from the high ground where they've been concealed up to this time."

Casca thought this over for a moment. "What of the other five thousand the King said would be here, and why didn't you mention them in your report?"

Indemeer sucked at his lower lip. "I didn't feel they were worth mentioning, considering what they are."

Casca rose from his chair, addressing not only Indemeer, but all of the officers present.

"When I say give me a status report it is not for you to determine what to delete. I alone will be the judge as to what is or is not important and any of you who think otherwise will not live to see the morning sun. Is that clear?"

He barked out the last question and the officers responded to the authority in his voice. They saluted and as one voice they cried out, "It is clear, Commander!"

Casca sat back down. "Now, where are the five thousand the King sent?"

Now thoroughly chastened, Indemeer pointed to an area just outside their encampment.

"There, Lord. They are under guard and have so far presented us with no difficulties." Casca asked him if they'd been told of their purpose in being brought to this place of battle, and of what they were to do.

Indemeer replied that all had been carefully instructed in what was expected of them and what their fate would be if even one failed to obey.

"Good! You've done well. But . . ." Casca touched the valley on the map that Indemeer had previously indicated as the engagement area. "Here is not where we will meet the enemy. From what you've told me about the rate of march of the Huns, they should be camped at least twenty miles from the mouth of the valley by the time we take up positions. No, we are going to meet them here." He indicated another, more narrow valley less than half a day's march from where they were presently encamped. "Here is where we will meet them, and not at the front of the valley but at the end of it. We shall make them come to us."

Indemeer started to protest but stopped at Casca's upraised hand.

"It will be here! By the time they reach this place they will have ridden all day, their animals will be tired and so will the men, giving us just a little more in our favor, and *Mithra* . . ." he paused and changed the god's name, after clearing his throat, "uh, *Ahura-mazda* knows we'll need all the advantages we can get should anything go wrong. In addition, our troops will be fresh and if your map is correct, the narrow confines of this valley will reduce the number of men that the Huns will be able to amass on their front at the charge. Then . . . if we can stop them and hold them and throw their front rank into a panic, the rest of the Hun force will be compelled to back up behind them, creating congestion and confusion—confusion that we'll be able to use to our own good purpose. As to the exact disposition of our forces, I will wait until I have seen the site before I make that decision."

Indemeer sucked at his lower lip again, but this time when he spoke his voice contained tones of respect. This organized plan was better than his own and the wisdom of tiring the Huns out while their own forces remained fresh was obviously to their advantage.

"Do you have anything further, Lord?"

Casca spoke, standing now. "Introduce me to your officers. I will entertain input from each as to anything that may hinder us in our mission. I wish to know the condition of not only your men, but also the animals and the pack train. Is the morale good or bad? What do the troops grumble at other than having me as their new commander?"

The officers looked at each other. The foreigner was no fool and spoke bluntly. Their basic hostility toward him began to change to that of professional respect. Regardless of where their new commander had come from, it appeared that he knew his business and theirs. They would obey now without the reluctance they'd felt earlier. Their new leader was a true warrior.

The night dragged on to the early hours as each officer in turn was questioned in detail and asked to contribute ideas that would possibly modify the commander's basic plan. It was dawn before Casca dismissed the last of them. Indemeer had stayed with him throughout the interrogations, making sound comments and judgments, familiarizing Casca with various problems each unit had faced on their arrival, each unit's history in battle, and a thumbnail profile of the unit leaders' histories and backgrounds. When they called it a night, both he and Casca felt they had put in a good day's work and were each more satisfied with the other as soldiers.

Two days and battle would be joined. Casca gave the order to break camp and move to the valley of his choice. The sooner they arrived the more rested his men would be when the time came for battle. He decided not to visit the five thousand men sent to him by Shapur. Those he would save until just before the engagement. He was confident now, after listening to Indemeer, that things would be as he'd said. But still he'd check on them personally now and then until it was time for them to be used.

FIVE

Casca surveyed the Persian Host. Twenty thousand men, one quarter of their ranks from Shapur's own bodyguard. The Immortals, each especially selected and trained, every man richly equipped with the finest of blades and armor made of steel scales that rippled in the day's sunlight.

The infantry stood at ease, weapons to hand, waiting for the appearance of the Huns. Casca had chosen this ground and gave the order to wait. They would move no further. By waiting here it would force the enemy to come to them, forcing them to march through the worst heat of the day, and when they did meet, a portion of their vitality would have been sapped by the Persian sun that baked the rocks of this valley until they split and cracked from the constant heating and cooling. He signaled his trumpeter, who responded with two short blasts. Five thousand men advanced from the rear to stand in five ranks in front of the rest of the waiting army of select troops. Now they totaled twenty-five thousand. These men were uniformed as the others, but carried no shields or spears; neither did they wear helmets of brass and iron.

Only the green tunics fringed with tassels identified them as members of the same force.

Rising, Casca removed his helmet and swung up into the saddle of his waiting horse, looking out over the five thousand. Filling his lungs, he called out to them.

"The King Shapur has given you this opportunity to save your families from death. You have already been sentenced to die, some of you for treason, others for robbery or murder or refusing to accept the state religion. It matters not what your crime against the Great King was, you are all as one in your sentence. But this day you shall be permitted to atone for those crimes and the Great King will spare your families. They will not have to go under the headman's ax. Let not one of you hesitate. Do as you have been ordered and all will be well for those you leave behind. Such is the order of the Great King."

Each of the five thousand raised his only weapon, a single knife, in salute and bowed low at the words of the Great King, Shapur.

Casca turned from them and returned to his position on the ridge to await the Hunnish horde.

What he had just done had not been an easy thing. He wished now that he hadn't told Shapur of the manner by which the Viscount of Wu had achieved victory over the Ch'u seven hundred years before with the use of three thousand men. But he had told him and Shapur had ordered him to try to same technique in this battle. Shapur, in his mind superior to any Chinese, had given Casca five thousand instead of the three used by the Viscount.

The only consolation he could muster for the

plan was that these men were already condemned and most of them would die this day with less pain than they would have if left to the tender mercies of the royal headsmen who delighted in their own forms of experimentation. And, Casca knew, Shapur's word was law. Their families would be spared. He had explained to Shapur that it would make the men accept their fate more easily and the King had conceded.

The five thousand men stood waiting in five ranks across the sunbaked floor of the valley, each to his own thoughts and fears. They knew they had no choice but to obey. They shuffled their feet nervously, the sun pounding on their temples and backs. Many already had the look of men dead, or at least men at peace with themselves. In their faces, Casca could see no panic. Fear, yes. Fear of the unknown. Some of them, in a perverse manner, even seemed to be looking forward to what the next minutes would bring.

At the far entrance to the valley the horsemen of the Hephalites began to gather, a cloud of dust rising over them as their horses milled about in their thousands.

War drums began to beat and the Huns sang and chanted as their shaman prayed to the elemental spirits. They whipped themselves into a fighting frenzy, ragged and savage apparitions, their horses wild, red-eyed and rearing, white streaks of foam dripping from their mouths and down their flanks. It was rumored that the Huns often fed their horses the flesh and blood of humans. Their Khans waited also, waited for the precise moment when their men were so filled with the lust to kill that they could no longer be restrained.

Now, horns blared. Under the horse-tailed standards, the Huns charged against the stationary line of the waiting Persians.

The first line of the five thousand condemned men stepped forward ten paces, separating themselves from the rest of the Host. They stood alone, without shields or spears to protect them, with only their short bare blades held above their heads, waiting for the Huns to close. Casca watched from his vantage point, feeling a little sick to his stomach. He couldn't let the Huns get too close or their own impetus would carry them through the first line. His trumpeter stood close by. Closer and closer the Huns advanced, the bravest of them on the fastest horses at the forefront, screaming.

The heads of vanquished enemies hung on ropes, draped from the necks of their foam-mouthed, red-eyed war horses. Closer, the drumming hooves came. Casca raised his sword, holding it above his head for a moment, the midday sun twinkling off the polished steel of its blade.

Now! He swung the blade downward and his trumpeter sounded a long single note to echo across the sun-bleached rocks of the valley floor. At the signal, the first rank of the condemned stepped forward two more paces and raised a single cry to the glory of the King of Kings, Shapur, then sliced their own throats open. In less than the beat of a heart, a thousand men cut their own throats in front of their Hunnish enemies and fell forward in their own blood.

The leaders of the advancing Huns slowed their charge. The horn sounded again and another thousand stepped forward to where the first had died, raised their knives in salute to Shapur, then sliced wide open their windpipes and fell across the bodies of those already dead.

The first wave of the Huns halted altogether. The smell of blood reached the flaring, foam-flecked nostrils of their steeds. Once more, then again. . . . And again, the lone signal of the trumpeter called forth a thousand to their death until the five thousand lay dead by their own hands. The Huns wavered; superstitious fear told them that this was something outside their experience. Killing the enemy they were used to, but an enemy who killed himself while shouting to the glory of his king was more than their barbaric mind could comprehend. And what one cannot understand, one fears. And, behind the five thousand dead waited thousands more.

Basic primeval fear of the unknown rushed over them as the remaining forces of the Persian Host raised their lances and spears on high and cried out in the Hunnish tongue as Casca had taught them. "Death! Death! Death!"

The Huns broke, and turning back from the madmen they raced to the rear; for it was well known that the mad were protected by the spirits and to touch them was to invite disaster and death. They fled from the field, pursued by the Persian Cavalry. Having the fresh animals, the Persians quickly overtook the panic-stricken Huns whose horses even now were staggering and windblown. Some dying from ruptured hearts were throwing their twisted-legged masters to the earth where the Persian infantry quickly dispatched them. Among those whose animals could still run, panic spread as wildfire feeds on dry grass. Nothing could stop them but death. They raced to get away from the insane suicides.

Casca didn't join in the battle; there was no need. When the Huns broke, he knew then that it wouldn't be a fight, but a slaughter. And slaughter it was. All that day and into the dark, the Persian Cavalry pursued the Huns.

The following morning they counted the heads taken in battle. It required two hundred carts to carry the twenty thousand gape-mouthed trophies back to Nev-Shapur.

The Khans and Toumans of the Huns would think long and hard before they came again to the lands of the Sassanid kings. A nation that doesn't hesitate to kill itself is an enemy to be avoided. Besides, there were always easier pickings elsewhere.

SIX

The bloody business over with, Casca turned command of the Persian forces over to Indemeer and told him that he was returning to Nev-Shapur.

Indemeer bowed, accepting the responsibility and advising Casca that it would be wise to have a strong escort in his return. Many of the Huns that had escaped were now broken up into parties of varying sizes and scattered to the winds. There could be some behind them and it would probably be, Indemeer warned, at least a week or two before the last Hunnish forces could be rounded up and wiped out.

Casca agreed and Indemeer assigned a detachment of two hundred light archers to escort him back to the capital. The archers were under the command of young Shirkin who had not, as of yet, the full-grown beard favored by the Persians. It would still be a year or two before the dark fuzz turned into a proper growth. But Casca had noticed the young officer in battle. The youth had displayed a cool mind.

He had husbanded his forces and kept them from overextending themselves and being cut off from the main body. His courage was evident from the number of minor wounds he had received in the fight. His left arm, Casca could see, was nursing a saber cut almost to the bone and Casca knew the youngster had experienced agony from the red-hot iron used to cauterize the wound and keep it from corrupting.

Shirkin's face showed no sign of fever. His eyes were clear, though he did wince from pain now and then when his horse made too sudden a move.

They left the valley in formation, with scouts and skirmishers out. Half of their small force was utilized in this capacity while the rest rode in two ranks along the road. At midday they switched off, the outriders coming in to take up the ranks on the road while their comrades took their turn out front among the rocks and barren ground. Even when they switched it was not done all at once. In turn, one element would come in, then another. This way, they could not be caught by surprise with all their forces on the road and no scouts out.

As they rode from the place of slaughter they could see birds by the thousands flying over them, heading back from where the riders had come. Kites and vultures. Somehow they knew that ahead lay a place where food could be had. Even packs of jackals could be seen furtively scurrying between the scrub brush and rocks, making for the feast. Casca knew that before two days had passed there would be nothing left of the Huns' remains but scraps of cloth, fur, and scattered bones to whiten in the sun.

One of the outriders came at a gallop, his horse lathering at the chest and mouth. He reined up in front of Casca and Shirkin.

"Lord, I have sighted a band of Huns heading to the north of us. I think they are making for the river crossing."

"How many?" Shirkin beat Casca to the question.

"Perhaps as many as we, not more."

Shirkin turned eagerly to Casca. "How say you, my Lord? Do we pursue the beasts?"

Casca thought it over. "No! We'll let them go this time."

The messenger spoke again. "Forgive me, Lord, but the savages have already laid waste one village in their path and have slain all there. Even the old men and babes. And Lord, there lie at least two other villages in their path before they reach the river. Will you leave your people to face them alone?"

Casca had seen the handiwork of the Hunnish tribes too many times not to know what anyone who came across them would face, and death, he knew, would be the least of the agonies. Raising up in his saddle, he called:

"Bring in the flankers and scouts, we ride north!"

Shirkin cheered at the words, as did all in hearing range of Casca's voice. They turned the column northward, riding swiftly. Casca made them alternately get down from their horses and run along beside them while hanging on to the saddle straps or to the horse's tail. This would give the animals rest from the weight on their backs, and though not as fast as riding constantly, Casca knew from experience that they would more than make up for it in the long run by covering more distance and still having fresher mounts when they needed them.

By sundown they had come across one of the villages previously visited by the Huns. The sweet stench of death greeted Casca's small force. All were dead. What the scout had said about the other village was also true here. Men, women, and children had all been slaughtered. The Huns had obviously rounded up everyone and herded them into the center of the small village, and there had methodically cut every person's throat. Even the babes, lying still now beside their mothers, had not been spared. It was a scene like this that, more than anything else, always brought the black urge to kill over the Roman. And as they rode on, the hate grew with each league as they closed in on their quarry.

All that night they rode, eating and sleeping in the saddle. By dawn, they knew they were very close. The droppings from the Hun's mounts in front of them were still damp and steaming. They were only minutes behind them now and Casca, red-eyed and angry, wanted them badly.

He hadn't fought in the battle in the valley. There'd been no need. But this was one he would not miss out on and his sword would be needed. They crested a rise and Casca called a halt. Below, crossing a small plain, were the Huns, strung out in a ragged line. Their numbers, as his scout had estimated, were about equal.

Wondering how to catch up with the Huns, Casca noticed the enemy would be forced to cross a large field of high grass, shimmering yellow now in the morning light, thigh high to a man.

Casca called to Shirkin to send him four riders and a spare mount for each. He explained his plan for stopping the Huns to Shirkin and the youngster grinned in boyish glee.

"As you command, Lord." Shirkin gave the orders and the four light archers sped off to the side of the rise, riding as though there would be no tomorrow. Whipping their horses, they raced the already tired animals, leading their spare mounts by lead ropes. About halfway to the field of grass, as Casca watched, they leapt first one, then another, from the backs of the spent horses onto their spares, releasing the tired animals and whipping the others onward. They passed the Huns, who were staring at them in wonder. The riders were too fast and the Huns let them pass without trying to give chase. They and their horses were too tired and besides, what danger could four lone riders represent when they were this near to the river crossing and there were no Persians ahead.

The Persian riders raced on into the highest part of the grass, disappearing from sight. Casca waited impatiently. He didn't let his horsemen leave the heights, not wanting to give the Huns any more to alarm them.

Shirkin pointed with his drawn sword. "There, my Lord! They have started!"

From the grass came one lone tendril of smoke, and then another. In ten minutes, the entire field of grass was one solid line of flames in front of the Huns. At this precise moment, Casca gave the order to form and advance.

The wind was blowing in their direction, into their faces and those of the Huns, but the Huns' attentions were focused on the sea of fire before them; their tired, frightened animals whinnied and shied at the crackling roar of the flames. They halted now to wait out the fire. From where they were situated, the Huns knew the flames couldn't reach them and would burn themselves out without too much trouble. All they had to do was wait. Many of them took this opportunity to dismount and take a leak or a crap while squatting beside their mounts. Several were still in this awkward position when the first arrows of Casca's archers reached them.

The wisdom Casca had shown in having his men give the horses a break while running beside them proved its value now. His men were tired from the forced ride, but the memory of what they'd seen in the village had been riding with them. It gave them the needed factor to drive down on the rear of their ancient enemy. Hate drove them, hate so strong that it drove away fear of their own deaths.

The Huns were still strung out in a single ragged line up to the edge of the grass. Casca and his warriors swept down and over them, rolling them up a few at a time as they hit en masse.

Casca left the use of the bow to his Persian archers, who were much more proficient in shooting from the saddle than he himself was, and used only his sword. The longer Persian blade proved its merit over the Roman short sword by giving him a longer reach, which he used to good advantage. The strength of his swing was aided by the movement of his horse. His blade flashed again and again, and with each stroke a Hun went down minus his head, the body standing momentarily before falling to lie twitching in death on the ground.

About one half of the Huns had managed to gather in force, their backs against the searing wall of flames, grass smoke swirling about them, gray clouds stinging their eyes and sending their mounts into a state of frenzy. Only the strong hands of their masters kept them from bolting and running wild.

The Persians drew up in line, facing their enemies. Both sides had bows drawn and arrows notched, waiting for what both sides knew would be death.

The horses of each side stood, legs wobbly, their flanks heaving. No word was spoken. Only the crackling of the raging grass fire made noticeable sound.

They waited, each side trying to gather its strength. One of the Huns in the line threw back his head and, face to the sky, he held his sword to the heavens and began to sing, a strange gutteral cry, rising and falling. He was calling upon the primal spirits of the earth and sky to accept him. The others took up the death cry in unison and the Huns prepared to die.

To Casca's ear, the combined voices of the Huns were not unlike the howling wail of wolves. The final note of the death song faded. Small fires flared up, then died under the stamping hooves of the horses. Smoke bit at their eyes, causing tears to run freely from the eyes of the Persians as well as from those of their foe. They waited, both sides crying, the moment tense while each watched the other. Then, at an unspoken command, the Huns broke and charged. The wild creatures of the steppes whipped their flagging beasts into a ragged gallop. The Persians waited until only a hundred feet separated them, then raised their bows and fired. The arrows, streaking single shafts of death, glided through the air to find their targets. The Huns went down under the rain of wooden shafts and the Persians dropped their bows and drew swords to close in upon the survivors.

Casca raced the short distance with his men; blood pounding in his temples, face red from exertion, hands sweaty, the cords standing out in his neck, he struck again and again, the longer Persian blade reaching out to lay open the bellies or throats of all he could reach. One black, gap-toothed mouth after another disappeared in a mask of blood. The Huns gave no real resistance. They had in song conceded the fight before they'd charged. This was only their way of showing courage before death. And it came at the merciless hands of the Persian Cavalry. None were spared. Even the wounded horses of the Huns were put to the sword to lie kicking beside their bestial masters, who now in death seemed ridiculously harmless. They were merely dark, broken, bleeding clumps, spotting the ground in their filthy furs and leather trousers. Dark pools of their life source marked the spot where each lay, waiting for the birds and hungry jackals.

The Persians were now starting to take heads—trophies to take back with them—but Casca put a stop to it. He did not relish riding three hundred miles with the smell of rotting meat in his nostrils each step of the way. With some reluctance, his men obeyed and tossed the heads they'd collected back to the ground to lie mute on the stones of the plain's floor, eyes open, watching their killers.

Casca and his riders moved away from the killing ground, away from the smoke and mess of the grass fire to a spot by the river where they could rest and water themselves and their animals. Each of them took turns soaking their bodies in the waters of the Oxus, but only a couple of them ventured out farther than a few feet from the shore. The Persians were plainsmen or from the hill tribes and few knew the art of swimming.

Casca stripped to his loincloth and let the rushing waters rinse the smell of smoke and the stench of blood from his body. The sight of his scars and the knotted twisted muscles that rippled and turned with his every movement gave him new respect in the eyes of his warriors. Casca knew he was being watched and wondered if they would have liked to earn his muscles and scars the way he had, from years on the rowing benches of galleys. He had always been a relatively stout man, but the endless months of keeping time to the *horator's* beat had given him a strength in his wrists and back that only one who'd served likewise could have. He'd met stronger men than himself in his lifetime but they'd been few.

The water felt good. It eased the ache in his butt from days in the hard saddle. The inside of his thighs were rubbed sore. He knew the aching would pass soon and for now it was sheer luxury to just get off the damned mobile torture rack for awhile.

He gave the order to set up camp and for cooking fires to be lit. The horses were to be taken care of and put on a line where they could be fed and watched. Details were sent out to gather wood and to cut some of the high grass for use as fodder for the mounts.

Following this was the cleaning of all weapons and the cleaning of blood from their clothes. Good soldiers were sharp soldiers.

Here they would spend the night before the long journey back to Nev-Shapur. Rest had been well earned by these Persian warriors.

Casca slept fitfully, remembering the five thousand condemned men.

SEVEN

They rose from their beds before dawn and made ready to ride. The miles dropped rapidly behind them this time; there were no interruptions to their journey. The warriors, it seemed, were in good spirits. Even the wounded made little complaint about their injuries.

After two days' march, Casca decided to leave the wounded behind with a strong escort and move on ahead with only a few guards. They'd make even better time that way.

He and his guards ran into the survey party of Imhept the Egyptian. They were returning from surveying the flow of rivers to the north. With pleasure, Casca joined his own party with that of Imhept. He'd always been impressed with the quiet strength of the mild-mannered scholar.

The two men, a warrior and a scholar, passed the hours with ease. They had much to talk about. From Imhept, Casca learned many things about the ancient Egyptians. He learned of their gods and their religious beliefs, and of their ways of life. He was amazed at how many centuries the Egyptians had ruled as a power. It made the few centuries of

Roman rule seem pitifully short and from the looks of things, he couldn't see much possibility of Rome even coming close to the thousands of years that Imhept had told him of the dynastics of Egypt.

They were only a day's ride from Nev-Shapur when he called a halt for them to rest and clean themselves up a bit before going on. Also, it would give him a little more time with his newfound friend. Casca was really fond of the bald little man and he hoped that their individual duties would not keep them apart too often.

He was enjoying the brief respite from the trail as he and Imhept walked through the streets of a village close to their campsite. To both their delights, the annual festival was taking place there. Casca had wondered about the number of tents and yurts that were scattered around the outskirts of the village, but had thought at the time that it might just be a time for trading or census that had brought so many tribesmen in from the desert and mountains.

That was part of it, too, but the real reason was the holding of the annual *Buzkash* during the festival. He had never seen one before, but he was aware that the wild tribesmen of the north were heavily addicted to the sport. The villagers, being lowlanders, didn't participate in the game and Casca didn't blame them. It looked damned rough, and dangerous as well, to a man's health.

From what he had seen so far, he figured that the idea was basically this: two sides mounted up and faced each other around the carcass of a decapitated calf on the ground. Then they would proceed to have a free-for-all. One side would grab the carcass and try to race around the field to a marked spot and set it down before the competition could take it away from them. It sounded simple enough until you realized that either side could use anything other than knives and swords to get the damned thing away from your team. This included ramming one another with their horses, hitting with fists, and lashing the others with short riding crops.

It was not unusual for two or three men from each team to be killed, or at least crippled, in each event. Each event was settled through a process of elimination as to who was the victor. The prizes varied each time. A horse this time, a slave girl the next. The nomads all had one thing in common: they were proud, fierce men who took offense easily and normally spent most of their time either robbing or killing one another, but during the festival of the *Buzkash,* there would be no fighting among themselves, except on the field. In their faces he saw traces of the Mongol mingled with the fair hair and blue eyes of the Kushanites, who claimed they were the descendents of the armies of Alexander.

In the open-air market place, the vendors cried out for the noble lords to see and buy their goods. Everything was for sale, even their women. Casca was tempted but rejected the women, mostly because he didn't wish to offend the sensibilities of his companion.

They had made their own camp and Casca regretted that they had no baths. But he would at least wipe the worst of the trail dust from him and have his uniform taken to the stream where it would be stone-pounded and washed by a couple of the village women. It wouldn't help much, but it would perhaps remove a little of the sour smell of overheated horse and stale blood from it.

While this was being accomplished, he lay around in the shade in his loincloth, enjoying an evening breeze that helped to cool his body and diminish some of the aches of battle and days in the saddle. He regretted that he would once again have to climb back into the saddle the next morning. But there was nothing to be done about it; he had to report in. This side trip meant that he was already late, and surely by now Shapur had word of the battle and was wondering where in the hell his general was. Casca didn't want to piss off his king and knew that Shapur had short reins on his temper. But if Shapur would give him time to explain the reasons for his delay, he was sure the king would approve.

That night, he and Imhept sat by their campfire listening to the chanting of the tribesmen and the beating of their drums. Each, it seemed, was trying to be louder than the other. These, combined with reed flutes, mingled with the nasal, almost whistling trill of the village women in their black robes.

He and his companion fed on a spiced stew of young lamb and flat cakes of bread, toasted on hot stones. The meat was flavored with a trace of mint, which these people had a predilection for.

Imhept sat, facing Casca, wearing only his thin robe of linen. He didn't seem to mind the night chill at all, though Casca gave a shiver or two and tossed a couple of dried camel chips on the fire to warm things up a bit.

They sat up late that night and talked of things far away, of the minds of men and deeds men had accomplished and of gods and luck. The Egyptian's voice was low and patient, as if he were trying to give Casca the benefit of his years. Casca knew that it was strange he should feel so much younger than this small, pleasant man when, in actuality, he passed him by many years. But he had not the maturity of Imhept, maturity that comes with age and the peace of mind that comes with time. Perhaps that was part of his curse, too. He would be always what he was until the Second Coming. . . .

When Orion the Hunter passed over the clear night sky, they slept. Tomorrow they would both have to face Shapur again and that was not a chore to be relished under the best of circumstances.

It was near the evening hour when they finally arrived at the gates of Nev-Shapur the next day. The crowd was flowing outward, merchants and farmers returning to their homes. There was no place for them inside the walls after dark.

Casca led the way, acknowledging the salutes of the guards at the gate with an offhanded wave of his right arm. Once inside, he bade a temporary farewell to Imhept and the two of them went their separate ways, Imhept to his house and Casca directly to the palace.

He dismissed his guards at the entrance to the palace grounds, letting them return to their barracks to do the things all soldiers find pleasurable after a victory. To boast to their comrades and recount the deeds of their valor, deeds that would grow with each telling until their achievements rivaled the feats of the immortal gods of Olympus themselves.

For Casca, he had to face another power, one he found more fearsome than the gods of Greece and

Rome combined. They were only phantoms, designed to scare children, but Shapur could provide anyone that offended him with an immediate entrance to the gates of hell.

He was admitted to the palace by the majordomo, who looked with some distaste at his travel-stained apparel. Casca didn't really care whether the eunuch approved of him or not. He knew that his dress would not go against him, for Shapur was interested in results, not fancy clothes.

Passing through the same fresco-lined halls that he had entered on his first visit to the throne room, he tried to pull his thoughts together. He wanted to make the shortest and clearest report he possibly could. He reached the door to the throne room. On each side of the entrance stood the Immortals of Shapur's personal guard. Inwardly, Casca was amused at their titles. Immortals? If they only knew.

The massive doors swung wide and the majordomo turned Casca over to the chamberlain, who immediately announced his presence. Tapping his metal-tipped staff on the marble floor three times, he called out for all to hear and bear witness that Casca, sent by his sovereign lord, Shapur II, to wage war against the Hephalites, had returned.

Casca strode to the center of the hall and stood rigidly at attention, looking straight ahead. Shapur was seated on his alabaster throne, wearing, as was his usual habit, only simple, plain clothes. His only jewelry pieces were two bands of silver, set with turquoise, on his wrists. A single silver headband served as his crown and beared in his hand was the ever-present sword. He rose from his seat.

"Welcome, Lord Casca. I see you have returned

bearing your shield rather than sitting on it. May I presume that your campaign was successful?"

By his tone, Casca knew that he'd already received a full report from his agents on Casca's mission. Shapur spoke.

"Well, Lord Casca, how did our little ruse work? Did it perform as well for us as it did for the General of Chin?"

Casca admitted that the five thousand who'd slit their own throats had done good service and had fulfilled their end of the bargain.

Shapur was pleased. "Then I shall do likewise. Their crimes and dishonors are forgiven and their families shall bear no guilt. This is my word, so shall it be recorded."

Scribes hastened to put down his words of command, as Casca related the details of the battle, even though he knew that Shapur already had the information. He explained his delay in reporting back because of the raid he'd made on the Huns by the river. Shapur accepted his explanations and raised his sword, pointing it at him.

"Hear me well. This man has done our bidding and has returned victorious. Let none of you do otherwise. This warrior is in my favor and it shall be so noted and demonstrated by the fact that from this time on, he shall have the full rank of general. He shall also be granted a reward of three thousand pieces of silver and a talent of gold."

He addressed the entire hall. "Know ye full well, that I know how to reward those who obey as well as how to punish those that offend me. Mark this man's example. He came to our court as a stranger and is now honored and trusted by us. From this time on, no one shall refer to him as a foreigner, for by my word, he is accepted into our ranks. Casca, Baron of Khitai, and now general of my armies, is a Persian by my order. So it has been said, therefore it is done. For I am Shapur."

Casca bowed his way out of the royal presence and returned to his own residence to soak and scrape off the caked grime of the Persian deserts and plains. On his way out of the palace he was intercepted by Rasheed, who asked after his health and whether all was well with him. Rasheed had volunteered to give him whatever support he could in his position at court. His words were honeyed, but something told Casca that the flavor in back of them warranted his watching out.

Casca spent the next twenty-four hours sleeping the deep rest of exhaustion that comes when one has finally finished a long and tiring journey. When he awoke, he felt drugged, his head and limbs heavy and slow, his thoughts hard to gather. It took a few hours and some solid food, washed down with wine, before he could get his body moving properly.

It was near the twilight hour when, escorted by two of the household bodyguards, he ventured out into the streets. His personal bodyguards, he wondered? Or his jailers? He still wasn't quite sure of his status with Shapur. It didn't really matter.

He wandered into the market places, enjoying the freedom from the spine-jolting saddle he had ridden on for the last weeks, pleasuring himself at the stretching of his legs and being able to stop and sample fresh grapes from the mountains or wine from the vineyards of Armenia.

He passed the street of potters, their ever-spinning wheels being powered by naked feet, and made his way through a crowd of merchants and hawkers crying out for him to buy their wares.

He entered the grand bazaar, where the last slaves of the day were being offered for sale, and decided to watch the action for awhile. He had no intention of buying anyone, but he was curious to see what kind of merchandise was being offered on the block.

Slaves from many lands were available to those with the silver or gold to buy them. There were fair-haired Circassians, and even some wild men from the Colchis, where, it was said, that the legend of the Golden Fleece had its origin. The savages of the Colchis made the gathering of gold their principle occupation, supposedly, by placing sheepskins in the fast-flowing streams, the oily hair collecting the particles of gold being swept along.

The bidding was noisy, as the buyers, each with his own need, made offers on strong black males to work in the fields, or contractors, looking for cheap labor for the constant building programs they had received contracts on from Shapur's ministers. They all yelled out their bids loudly. Female slaves, several who were real beauties and proud of their bodies, twisted and turned, showing their charms, hoping to attract a wealthy purchaser who could give them at least a minimum of comfort, rather than the hovel of some goat herder who wanted a slut to slop his pigs and warm his bed.

The bidding was brisk but the prices, as near as Casca could see, were reasonable enough. A good looking wench was going for an average of fifty denarii or two gold solidii. Actually, not a bad price. Casca watched the women and was tempted to bid a couple of times, but restrained himself.

This suddenly changed, however, when the auctioneer brought his next offering on the block. Casca liked what he saw, even though the female slave was filthy and her hair was hanging in greasy, tangled tendrils. She was almost naked, her back showing the evidence of recent lashings, though none appeared to have been delivered with intent to permanently scar and would fade in a few days. She stood as a caged animal might, twisting and twitching in barely controlled rage. Her head would have scarcely reached Casca's shoulder and her breasts were small, though exceedingly well formed and ripe. The auctioneer made an effort to get her to move around the block so as to show off more of her charms, but every movement she made was of pure hate and resentment, and the buyers could tell, so bidding had not started.

The auctioneer tried to prod the bidding by claiming that she'd just recently been brought in and hadn't been in care long enough to be properly trained. He pointed with his rod to her legs and breasts, crying out to the noble lords to see how strong the limbs were, and how the high set of her breasts would surely delight any man of sensibility. Holding her face in his hand, he pried her mouth open with his rod, showing that her teeth were not as rotten as her disposition. He nearly lost a finger in the doing.

She stared at the would-be buyers with such open loathing that it was scaring them off. They wanted a good worker or a willing bed warmer, not some bitch who would stick a knife in them the first time they closed their eyes. And, there was little doubt in their minds that this would be the fate of the unfortunate sucker who could be conned into purchasing her.

Casca bid one silver coin of Darius. The auctioneer tried to raise the ante, crying for another bid. There was silence and Casca thought he'd bought her for the low price, but suddenly from the rear came another bid of two small gold coins. It was an Arab merchant in a turban and burnoose. The bidding between the two men became a contest, the woman was secondary now. When Casca and the Arab locked eyes there was instant dislike and each knew that the other would go the limit of his wealth, if for no other reason than sheer pigheadedness. The woman was no longer as important as the winning. Arabs were known to be great gamblers and losing at anything ate at their craws. The bidding continued to rise until Casca finally removed his purse and walked directly up to the block. Inside it, there were the last of the gemstones given him by Tzin. He poured them all into the palm of the auctioneer, a rainbow of colors, enough to make the auctioneer a wealthy man for the rest of his life—yet Casca was hoping that the greasy bastard would die before sundown.

The Arab gave up. To go against such a bid, that was even now being tallied by gem experts, would have broken him completely. He left the scene, his robes whipping about him angrily as Casca was handed the title to his new acquisition.

Casca asked the she-savage's name and whence she had come. He learned that she was Anobia and had been picked up on a slaving raid in the mountains of Armenia. That was all they knew of her and the auctioneer wished the foreign lord good luck with his purchase of the she-wolf. He was surely to need it. He asked Casca if he had a specific mark that he would like her branded with, so as to be more readily found if she should escape. Casca told him no, he wanted no more marks on her skin. Anobia said nothing, watching her new owner with contempt.

When he drew near, the smell of her almost drove him back. The auctioneer apologized, saying the wench refused to do anything and had badly scarred up a couple of his eunuchs when they had attempted to bathe her.

Casca took the rope leash, attached it to the slave ring around her neck, and jerked her from the stage without giving her a chance to do or say anything. Keeping the rope taut, he made his way amid the laughter of the crowd at his senseless purchase, and kept her well behind him so he wouldn't have to smell her. The bodyguards, who normally walked behind him, also moved to the front.

Now that he had her back in his rooms near the palace, he dismissed his guards. She stood in the center of the room, a wary, frightened animal, her eyes darting back and forth as if looking for a weapon. Casca ignored her; he knew what was going on in her mind. He ordered his household servants to draw water for the bath. While they did so, he changed into a more practical costume for the job forthcoming. Clad only in a loincloth, he walked back into the main room where she was still standing, her thighs quivering, a red mark on her neck from the tugging at her leash.

Anobia drew back, half frightened at the sight of the man in front of her, yet fascinated. She'd never seen a body with so many scars, and the body of her new master was a twisted, knotted mass of muscles in which the many scars left deep channels that made some of them move in manners they had not been designed for.

Casca stood directly in front of her and locked his eyes on hers, the gray-blue against the almond brown. He spoke to her now for the first time.

"Woman, you will wash yourself!"

She brought up some reserve courage, spitting at him. As soon as she'd spat, a hard hand knocked her to her knees, splitting her lip. He repeated his order.

"Woman, you will wash! I am not a *castrato* that will tolerate your foul manners."

Anobia rushed at him, fingers like claws going for his eyes, only to find her wrist locked in a steel grip, her body twisted around and Casca's fist wrapped in her hair. He threw her quickly to the floor and dragged her by the greasy locks of her filthy head to where the tub was waiting. Since his slaves were afraid to touch her, he dismissed them as he stripped the few tattered pieces of clothing from her body.

He felt his breath catch as he saw her fully for the first time. She was like a panther, all female, rippling flesh with no trace of fat. Only her breasts bounced when she moved. She came only to his shoulder but all of her was ready to fight. By the hair, Casca raised her clear of the floor, her feet dangling. Now, unable to do anything to resist his efforts, he swung her almost absentmindedly over the side of the tub and into the water.

She immediately started to fight, struggling against his force. He quickly stopped this new effort by forcing her head under the water, holding her until he saw bubbles, then raising her for breath and repeating the action over and over until she was finally too weak for further resistance.

He washed her then, with his own hands, as he would have a baby, taking no liberties with her. He was sure and methodical as he first scrubbed her hair, rinsing out the grease, then beginning to work on her skin. After he'd removed the grime he rubbed it into a healthy glow.

In spite of herself, she began to relax. She was tired. It had been a long struggle since she'd been captured and she gave in to the unrelenting hands that were now becoming more gentle as she resisted less and let them do their job. Casca's hands kneaded and stroked, gently, with a sense of familiarity. She felt like a babe in these hands and he was treating her as such. Even when he washed her breasts, his heavily scarred hands displayed no feeling that he was enjoying her helplessness and, in a distant corner of her mind, this bothered her.

The bath was done. Casca raised her from the water and called for fresh jars to rinse her off. When this was done, a robe was brought to wrap around her nakedness and Casca showed her to a small side room where a pallet was laid out. He motioned for her to lie down. Again she tensed. This was to be it! He was going to take her now!

Once again, though, the scarred foreign warrior surprised her when he suddenly left the room, leaving her to lie alone on the pallet. From where she lay, she could see that he'd returned to his room and had now closed the curtain behind him.

Anobia was confused. Why had he bought her if he did not desire her? Why would he pay such a great price, then ignore her? Still confused, she was unaware of the moment when sleep came to her. Her eyes closed; she was tired, very tired. In spite of it all, the bath had taken some of the tension of her past ordeal from her body, and she slept.

Casca called for wine, then for lamps to be lit in the corners and on the table, before which he sat on cushions, trying to answer the same questions to himself that Anobia had previously pondered.

He sat alone all that night thinking and cursing himself. What was there about the woman? He knew she could be more trouble than she was worth. For the amount of money he'd spent on her he could have bought twenty beautiful good-tempered wenches that would have been delighted to serve him. But there was something! Was it the pride? She had continued to fight even though he'd known she was terrified. She'd fought in the only way she knew.

Dammit! I've no business getting emotionally involved with a woman. The only thing it ever brings me in the long run is pain. But still, there is something to her that cries out to me!

He peeked in on her a couple of times that night, fighting the temptation to enter and lie beside her. He knew he could take her if he wished, but he also knew that there would be scant pleasure in the taking, that she would give him nothing. He might enter her body, but that would be all. He could not touch her mind or her body in that fashion. He cursed himself again for wondering why that should make any difference to him. But it did.

Once, while she was sleeping, he'd seen her shivering from the night air and he had brought a coverlet, laying it gently over her, careful not to wake her as he watched her face in sleep. She was beautiful and probably had no more than twenty years of life to her. By the gods, he felt old, and he knew he was old, in ways that normal men could never understand. Old in the way that only trees or stones could know, and he had no business with feelings.

He knew she would be dust and he would still be the same. Time is a heavy burden when the sands run slow.

The night wore on. Casca dozed, still sitting by the table while the oil lamp threw shadows against the walls. He was there when dawn came.

Anobia awoke with a jerk, her eyes at first panicked. She removed the coverlet from her, wondering where it had come from. Rising, she unconsciously touched her hair and moved the curtain aside, walking to the room she'd seen Casca enter. She watched him for a moment before the rustling of the curtain aroused him. His eyes jerked wide open at the sound and immediately locked on hers. He nodded his head then. A decision had been made.

He motioned for her to come to him. She obeyed, walking slowly, stiff-legged, as a frightened fawn might. For there was power in this man. He motioned for her to kneel and she obeyed, wondering why she was not resisting his orders.

His rough hands reached ever so slowly around her neck and, with a twisting motion, his fingers tore apart the slave collar. Lying on the table was the deed the auctioneer had given him. He unrolled the document, took a stylus, and after making some marks on the scroll, signed his name and rank. Anobia watched, wondering. Wearily, he handed the document to her.

"Here, take it, woman. You're free. I will not have that which is not freely given and I feel that it is best if you leave this house and return to your own people. Surely you will give me nothing but pain if you stay."

In contrast to his rough handling of her the night before, these words were spoken gently. She knew that he'd wanted her and could have taken her. But he hadn't. Anobia put the document of her manumission inside her robe, saying nothing. She was confused in her mind.

Casca spoke again. "You're free to go woman."

She looked deeply into his eyes and she saw a difference. There was something inside them that she'd never seen in a man's eyes before. A terrible sadness, a loneliness that was a bottomless well of grief. These eyes, she knew, had seen more suffering than she would ever know. She saw something else in those eyes now, when he looked at her—the beginning of love was there. That was why he was setting her free. He was afraid of falling in love with her.

Casca waved his hand. "Go from me now!" He tossed her a sack of silver coins. "This will see you back to your people. Go! Leave me now!" He placed his head between his hands, elbows on the table, and would not look at her again.

Anobia rose silently, holding the bag of silver in her hands, and walked out of the door and into the streets of Nev-Shapur.

Casca sighed, letting the breath out slowly. His eyes were heavy. He laid his head on the table and slept again. She was gone.

A tinkling sound awoke him, his eyes heavy with unfinished sleep. The tinkling continued while his eyes struggled to focus on the table. He saw one small sparkle, then another and another as the coins fell in a pile before him.

Anobia was kneeling beside him. When the last coin fell from the pouch to join the others on the table, she dropped the bag atop them and touched his hand with her own, resting her small fingers on top of his. She spoke softly. "You are tired, my master. Come and lie down."

She had tried to leave, but something had drawn her back. Four times she had walked away only to find herself standing again and again in front of his doorway. So she'd returned, ignoring the questioning looks of those of his household. There was something she had to find out.

She took his hand; this time she did the leading as she guided him to her pallet. Heavily, he lay down and she put herself beside him, her heart beating wildly, her mind still confused at what she was doing. She waited for him to take her. She'd never had a man before. Though many had tried, she'd fought them all so savagely that they'd left her in search of easier pickings.

But now, she waited. She almost panicked and ran as his muscled arm went around her shoulder and drew her to him, but this arm was gentle and it was pulling her close into him and she wasn't running. Her head against his chest, her face against his skin, she waited for the hands to take her robe from her. But the hands never came. Casca slept, holding her to him as he would a child, and she finally relaxed, moving her face so that her hair was out of the way and her face and mouth were next to his chest. Then, she, too, slept. Slept in the arms of the man who'd bought her, then had sent her away. And with that sleep, she, too, fell in love with him. In some strange manner, his not taking her then, the possessive embrace, the closeness, had drawn her to him more than any other act ever could have.

They slept long and deeply, each next to the other. It was nightfall before they awakened and looked at each other, both surprised at what they saw in the other's eyes and face.

Casca kissed her. A long, deep gentle kiss that pulled her breath from her and then gave it back to her, along with his own. They joined and she opened up to him. The first pain was as nothing and it passed quickly. They loved each other. There was no rushing, no heavy thrusting or tearing. It was gentle, almost reluctant in the taking, and the tenderness this rough warrior had shown she never knew existed in men.

Shapur received word that his general had taken a slave girl and he was pleased. A woman served to slow a man down, and it would give him something else to use as leverage if the Roman should ever become troublesome for him and force a change in their relationship. He hoped the Roman would put the wench with child soon. That would tie him even stronger.

Anobia shared the King's wish to bear a child, but though she'd tried as hard as she could to have the seed of her man take place and grow, her womb remained empty. Nothing worked, not even the potions from the wise women. But still, the effort of trying was pleasing and not at all a wasted one.

Casca, for his part, enjoyed the attentions of his

woman. It was good to have a proper house to come home to. After months of campaigning in the deserts and mountains it gave him a feeling of permanence. He pushed from his mind the well-known fact that he would someday have to leave, content to enjoy the moments of peace and comfort that she could give him now.

He began to entertain a bit, not only the officers of his command, but also Imhept when he was available for good food and conversation. He enjoyed the old man's company more than any other. There was a timelessness to him as solid as the pyramids. Nothing ever seemed to rattle him. Imhept took all things calmly, as though he always had more important things to consider other than such mundane things as living, or work.

A few months after his arrival back in Nev-Shapur, Masuul, his housemaster, came to him to complain about Anobia. With quiet amusement, Casca listened to his tale of Anobia's extravagance. She had gone to the baths, then the hairdresser, then to the most expensive of dressmakers, and had even visited a house of the Hedria for a period of time. It was not to be tolerated for his master's woman to consort with known courtesans and people of ill-repute.

Casca listened to his servant's list of Anobia's transgressions patiently, telling him he would look into the matter. He was actually curious as to why Anobia would be spending time at the house of courtesans, but then he'd never been able to figure out why women did half of the things they did anyway, so why worry? He was content that she gave him pleasure and ease of mind and, if she was a little kinky, who the hell wasn't nowadays?

The answer to his question, as to why she'd been doing whatever the hell it was that she'd been doing, came to him the following evening.

When he'd returned from the training fields and entered the house, the servants informed him that she refused to come out to see him. She had remained in her room all day, not even coming out to eat, having her meals sent in. He tried to figure out what he'd done to upset her, giving it up as one of the mysteries of the female species. He wondered if women were truly of the same origin as men; they sure as hell didn't act like it at times.

He was relaxing on the divan, sipping white wine from Parnessius, letting his mind go. The day had been a real bitch and he was worn out. For the past three weeks he had been trying to instill some semblance of discipline into a batch of raw recruits from the provinces and tribute states. About the only thing that the recruits had in common was a mutual hatred of one another and of their instructors. It had been necessary to have two of them given twenty strokes of the *bastinado* to make them see reason and obey. He winced at the remembrance of his own experiences of the thin whipping rods striking the soles of his feet while imprisoned in Jerusalem. Merely having the feet whipped didn't sound too bad, but the pain was unbelievable. More than fifty strokes and a man would probably never be able to walk again without limping. Unpleasant thoughts; he pushed them from his mind and took another sip of the clear white squeezings of the grape. Masuul's words of Anobia came again to his mind.

"*Ahhhhhh shit!*" It was bad enough to come home after a hard day and try to relax, let alone having to worry about what your damned woman might be up to. There was never any way of pleasing a woman. But, by the gods, when they wanted to be sweet there was nothing in the world like them to ease the pain in a man's mind and bring satisfaction to his soul. As far as he was concerned, women were both the blessing and the curse of man's existence.

A slight rustling sound interrupted his thought process.

Anobia had entered the room quietly. The reason for her strange behavior in the past weeks was now suddenly clear to him. She evidently had been preparing herself for this moment.

Casca had just taken a mouthful of wine when he'd turned to look and it had damned near went down the wrong pipe at the sight of her. Anobia had been spending her time not in a fit of temper, but preparing herself to please him.

Her hair was dressed in dark, oily, shimmering curls that dangled almost to her waist. Her eyes were accented with Kohl. The soles of her feet and the palms of her hands were reddened with henna. Gold and silver bracelets hung from her neck, wrists, and ankles; most of them set with tiny bells that tinkled softly as she walked.

She was wearing a costume that seemed vaguely familiar to Casca—scarves of fine colored gauze and silk draped in layers over her figure; a veil covering her face to the nose so that her eyes seemed too large for the face.

She moved her hands above her head; on the fingers were tiny brass cymbals. Gracefully, she struck them once, letting their chimes die away, then struck them again. Casca was spellbound. A thin piping came to him from outside, then was quickly joined by the sound of flutes and the tambour, accompanied by a sambar that twanged strange, almost melancholy, trills. The cymbals on her fingers had acted as a signal for the musicians on the patio to begin.

Anobia moved, her body twisting slowly, beginning now to dance. Casca gulped down half a mug of wine. This looked as if it was going to be one helluva show.

One of her veils came off, then another. She whirled by the incense brazier and dropped a dark, doughy ball of matter into the brass bowl. It immediately began to smoke.

He couldn't speak, his throat had suddenly contracted to the point of closure. He'd always considered her beautiful, but he'd never dreamed of her looking like this. He poured more wine in his mug.

The scarves, one by one, were removed. Emerald green, translucent and glowing, followed next by one of sky blue; each revealing a little more of her body as she danced to the Oriental strains of the music from the patio. She danced, slowly at first, then gaining in tempo until musky sweat glistened on her now half-bared breasts.

The smoke from the brazier, not unpleasant at all, was seeking its way into Casca's lungs, causing him to lose all perspective. Anobia was the only thing that was real now and she was dancing for him, giving herself to him in the only way she knew how. His mind moved with the music and the rhythm of her body. Another scarf dropped to the floor, to be kicked away by the tinkling bells at her ankle.

She dropped to her knees before him, swaying her upper torso back and forth, the sweat beginning to run freely down the valley of her breasts. Eyes closed, she made love to him. He reached to touch her but she was gone. The time was not now.

The fumes from the incense brazier filled his mind, distorting his surroundings, giving everything a surrealistic flavor. It was all unreal, but evidently . . . Casca was stoned out of his gourd!

As the last scarf fell to the floor, the chiming of the bells and the cymbal movement of her fingers ceased. Anobia was naked. Her body sweating, her breasts heaving from the effort of dance, she stood before her man for a moment, thighs quivering nervously.

The music stopped, the silence broken only by the beating of their hearts and the pounding of pulses in their temples.

Anobia came to him and they joined, a joining that took Casca to what he believed to be the paradise that the eastern mystics called Nirvana.

It was later on that night, as she lay next to him in sleep, that the memory came back to him. Salome! Anobia had performed the dance of the veils.

There were some months of leisure for him after the Battle of the Five Thousand, and he made the most of it, spending every hour he could steal with Anobia. But Shapur hadn't let him stay idle for long periods. There were always men to be trained and tactics and politics to be discussed.

Shapur had a healthy respect for Casca's mind and used him as a counterpoint to many of his advisors who only told him what they thought he'd want to hear.

Casca, it seemed to Shapur, had more balls than the rest and would tell it like it was, regardless of the outcome.

There were months of campaigning for the King. The borders of Persia were surrounded by hostile elements and Shapur made good use of Casca's experience, subduing one tribe after another.

Shapur had accompanied him once on a campaign all the way to the Indus River, where they'd faced elephants in battle for the first time. He had seen some of the monsters previously in the arenas of Rome, trained to execute prisoners condemned to die, either by picking them up in their trunks and bashing their victim's brains out, or by kneeling on them. The most popular method with the crowds was when the huge animals would impale their victims on their tusks and toss them high in the air.

Casca had heard that they only killed in one manner, and that was in the first method taught. If it was true, he didn't know, but it made very little difference anyway, the end result was still the same. Death. . . .

The beasts were frightening in combat, though. The warriors from the Indus Valley painted their elephants in various colors and mounted small fortresses on their backs where archers and spearmen were cached in relative safety. But once you got used to the big ugly mammoths they weren't nearly as dangerous as they looked and could easily be spooked by fire or smoke. They would turn on their own riders and trample them underfoot in their haste to escape.

That particular trip had also afforded him the opportunity of watching Shapur in action. The man was fearless, but in Casca's opinion, not foolhardy, and his sword was as good as any he'd seen, even among the professionals of the Arena. Shapur was a craftsman, and Casca had his doubts about whether he could hold his own with this King of Kings. He was certain, however, that if the fight lasted for any length of time his reserves of strength would eventually give him an edge on Shapur, but he still wouldn't relish facing him one-on-one.

While others around him killed in rage or passion, Shapur went about the act like a man cutting off the heads of chickens for his dinner. He was nothing but pure business. Casca wondered! What did give the King pleasure?

Shapur had only gone on the trip to allow his men to see him in action and know that he was a fit and able king; that, and to keep an eye on Casca in person. He'd heard too many reports of the Roman's growing popularity. Not that he considered Casca any real threat to his throne, but there were events about to take place that could give the Roman the opportunity to make a certain degree of trouble for him if he wished, and the wise general always had plans laid for any contingency.

Yes, as they said, war was hell. But at least he had someone to return to—a good woman and a place offering gentle contrast to the horrors of war.

Anobia gave him peace of mind and soul when he needed it most and it was good to be able to return home and lose himself for awhile.

But he knew each period of rest and peace would be broken in time by the heavy-handed knock of an Imperial messenger. They would beat on his door in the wee hours of the morning, summoning him with bad news to Shapur's side. Why did bad news always come at night?

The seasons turned one after another, winter came and went, and he was pleased with life. He had respect and power, wealth and honors, and, above all else, he was loved.

Sometimes, when he thought of the old Jew, Samuel's warnings that Persia was not for the likes of a man like Casca, he would laugh. Hell, Persia was the best thing that had happened to him in a long time, and he was content.

His peace was interrupted again in late spring. This time the messenger's knock on his door came at a very critical time—he and Anobia were joined and Casca was approaching the area called the short rows. Damn!

Instinctively, he knew there was trouble. His sword was needed again by his king, Shapur.

EIGHT

From the rise, he could see the snaking line of his soldiers, twisting through the pass below him, laboring their way to the heights. Ten thousand warriors. Archers, light cavalrymen on horseback, and two thousand infantry. The men were leading their animals over the treacherous rocks and through places where the trail diminished in size to a width so narrow that the horses' bellies rubbed the rock walls.

Soon, they would start heading back down, down to where the air would be thick again and the men wouldn't have to gasp for breath every other minute.

Casca knew that on the other side of these mountains lay plush green valleys with plentiful fodder for their horses and fresh food for his men. At this rarified altitude, it was seldom that you could find anything other than moss or lichens that were stubbornly trying to eke out an existence on the granite face of the windswept rocks.

He had removed his helmet and tied it to his saddle. Cool wind came from the peaks to rustle through his hair. It was odd how a man could build up such a sweat in a location like this, with air cold enough that even now, in the heart of summer, breath was misting from the horse's nostrils at high noon. A distant scream came to his ears.

Another of his Persian warriors had lost his footing and had plummeted down thousands of feet, to smash on the rocky bed of the gorge below. Too bad. But they had been lucky, all in all. Only eleven men and ten horses had slipped today, but it had been enough to make the others wary and had slowed their movement. Casca yelled down for his commanders to speed their men up a little. He didn't have time to exercise as much caution as he would have liked. They must hurry. Twenty thousand Huns were up ahead, laying waste to Kushan, an ally and tribute state of Persia, and the gateway to the Indus and China.

It was there that Jugotai, as a boy, had served as his guide some forty years before.

Jugotai! A child then, but determined to be a man before his time. It had been he that had led Casca over this same mountain pass to safety. The raging torrents of winter wind and snow had kept them penned up for days in a small cave. It was easier this time.

His reflections were interrupted by the arrival now of Indemeer. The hoary old warhorse had insisted on coming with them on this mission. Casca knew the climb had been hard on Indemeer. The thin air had left his face flushed with white spots at the cheeks, but he would show no sign of visible difficulty to his men or his leader. Still, Casca thought, he had seemed relieved when he'd told him they were nearing the summit and for him to go on ahead of them and check the trail. Casca knew that this would get him on the other side first and down into thicker air, where the old man could breathe a little better.

As the lead element of archers passed him, he dismounted. Taking his horse's reins in the manner of his men, he walked the animal carefully over the loose stones and patches of ice remaining from the last storms of winter. Raising his eyes, he looked up even higher. The bare, craggy peaks wore only their eternal coat of ice and snow, standing out in stark contrast to the pale blue of the sky, fading into varying hues of purple and blue with the distance.

He reached the crest. Somewhere behind him, he knew, was the cave that he and Jugotai had stayed in, but he had not seen it on this trip up. Perhaps it had been concealed by one of the countless rockslides that plagued these hellish peaks.

In the distance, he could see the broad back of Indemeer just disappearing around a curve in the mountain. He'd started down now, and wasn't wasting any time in doing so. He figured the old soldier would reach the base of the mountain before nightfall. It was much shorter going down than coming up. They would only have to drop four or five thousand feet to reach the valleys of the highlands of Kushan. On the Persian side, the one they just came up, they'd had to climb over twelve thousand feet to reach the top of the pass. It had taken them four days.

He wondered if he'd ever meet Jugotai and his son, Shuvar, again, or even if they still lived. Jugotai would be old now, for a man of the hills anyway, and if he had survived the many battles with the rapacious Huns, he would certainly look much older than Casca. How would he explain that to Jugotai? What would he say to him about that? He shook off the thought. Time to worry about that when they met, if they met.

The trail had widened enough to accommodate horse and rider now. He threw his leg up and settled himself uncomfortably in the saddle.

He jerked and swayed down the trail until he came upon Indemeer. The old man rested against a large boulder, a skin of water in his hands, beads of perspiration rolling off his face. The white spots on his cheeks were gone now and color was slowly returning to his face. Casca was unsure if the old fellow would be able to make the return trip over the mountain behind them. But he was certain that the old bastard would try.

Indemeer waved him over, offering him his water skin. Casca dismounted, thinking that after this campaign he would find a good excuse to send Indemeer and a detachment of his best soldiers back home via the long route on the silk road. It would be longer, but easier on the old sucker.

He took the offered skin and uncorked it, taking a long pull. It was a flat, tepid fluid and it tasted of sweat. They would have fresh drink soon. Indemeer pointed down the trail.

"Not much farther, Lord. We should be there in an hour at the most."

Casca agreed with him, and they talked about what they'd do when they arrived. They knew when they reached the valley below that they would be at their most vulnerable. The troops would be coming down the pass in single file and exhausted from the labor of the climb. If the Huns were aware of their coming, and had sent a strong force to intercept them, they could keep the

Persians bottled up in the pass and pick them off a few at a time as they entered the valley. It was not a good position for an army to be in, but they had no choice in the matter.

A message, sent by a relay team of Imperial riders, had reached the court at Nev-Shapur ten days previously, saying that the city of Kushan was under siege. This had happened at the same time that the Kushanite armies were already engaged in a critical battle against the savage tribes to their far south, and there was no way that their forces could be disengaged without suffering terrible losses. If they withdrew, the enemy would surely pursue. The Kushanites could not possibly have withstood the attack of the combined forces of the tribes of Hind and those of the Huns should they decide to ally, so Casca had been ordered by Shapur to take his relief column of ten thousand soldiers to the support of the Kushanites in their struggle with the Huns.

He gave the lead element time to rest before sending them ahead to scout the terrain, checking for Hun patrols or units in that area. If none were sighted, they were to send back a rider; then the rest of the army would go down and make camp in the valley. If Huns were spotted, and depending on how many, he would decide what to do about that when the time came. Contingency planning was not his forte. He was a soldier of spontaneity, quick decisions on the spot.

In the meantime, it was good to rest and let the men take a break until the scout returned.

Indemeer leaned his gray, curled hair against the boulder, asking wearily, "How long ago was it, Lord, that you came over these foul passes?"

Casca thought carefully before answering.

"What is time to a place like this, old one? Let it suffice to say that it was longer than I'd like to think about. But to my eye, nothing has changed in these mountains since then."

Indemeer accepted the answer and changed his questions to the subject of the Huns ahead, and what their disposition should be in the relief of the Kushanite city. Casca didn't have answers to these either, saying only that they would wait and see. But if the Huns hadn't taken the city yet, it could be possible to trap them between Casca's men and the defending force of the Kushanites. If they could herd them up to the walls, where their horses would be of little use, the archers would be able to thin them out before closing in for the kill.

The scout returned, leaping from his sweating horse, and bowed to Casca.

"Lord, the way is clear ahead. There is no sign of the enemy, or that they have come this way."

Casca rose, addressing himself to Indemeer. "This is good. You go on down and select a campsite. I'll give the order for the rest of the army to get a move on. We'll have to spend at least two nights there to give the trailing element time to get down and for the horses to rest."

Indemeer raised his old bones from his comfortable rock and mounted his horse in obeyance of Casca's orders.

Casca called out to the approaching column for them to pass word back that they would be out of the mountains this night and camped in the green fields below. He could hear the cheers of elation as he moved to head the lead element, now preparing to move out.

NINE

Camp was made, pickets set out, and scouts sent far away to keep watch for any signs that the Huns were approaching their camp area.

Casca ordered that there would be no campfires that night. For as long as possible, he wanted the Huns to be unaware of their presence. Still, he knew that a warm meal was important for the morale of his troops, so he let the cooks remain at the foot of the pass with their cooking pots. The winds there would whisk away any smoke and the fires could be well concealed in the boulders. One detachment of men at a time, they made their way to the cooking area to fill their bowls and eat. It wasn't as good as the men would have liked, but it was better than cold mutton and bread.

Casca had the men set his command tent up near the pond where he and Jugotai had rested on their way to Kushan. He walked the picket line twice that night to assure himself that none of his sentries were sleeping on duty. Twice, his outriders had come back in to report. They had seen nothing other than a giant glow on the horizon, probably a burning village, he thought.

Casca checked in on Indemeer to see how the old

man was faring. Indemeer's face had regained most of its color and he seemed to be breathing much easier. Casca was relieved; he liked the old warhorse a lot, and needed him and his support. Indemeer lazily asked of Casca how much farther they had to go before reaching Kushan.

"Four, perhaps five days at the most, old friend. From here on in we go in triple columns, as long as the terrain permits, that is. I don't want us to get strung out to the point that there's a possibility that our lead or trailing elements could be cut off."

He knew the Huns were skilled at the old tactic of attacking the leading element and then, when the rear rushed up in aid of their comrades, the Huns would desist and wait for them to spread out again, attacking the rear next and forcing the front to double back and give assistance. These tactics caused considerable wear and tear on the men and the animals and could slow a march nearly to a standstill. By using three lines of march he would be able to counter an attack without having his men rushing back and forth. If one line was assaulted they would fall back on their nearest supporting line. Should the Huns be stupid enough to attack between the columns, they'd be trapped inside. Indemeer nodded, smiling in admiration of his commander's battle savvy. Casca bade him to have a good night.

The order of march, when they broke camp the following morning, was as he'd told Indemeer. His officers listened, making suggestions. Some were accepted, some were not. The hundred small details of any army somehow sorted themselves out when they moved.

Three weaving tendrils of men and animals moved through the valley floor towards Kushan. Casca had the infantry hold to the tails of the horses to help pull them along. This would increase their distance and, with a little practice, they would be able to cover thirty or even forty miles a day, depending on the terrain.

Casca took up a position in the center line while Indemeer commanded the left. The right file was led by the young officer, Shirkin, who had accompanied Casca on his first encounter with the Huns under the standards of Shapur. Casca had promoted him to the rank of regimental commander after that battle, pissing off some of the senior officers. But Casca knew the young man's capabilities and he also wanted a few reliable men around him that owed him a debt of gratitude. He'd much rather have someone on his side that served out of loyalty rather than just being paid for their services.

Three times on the march, they came across evidence of the Huns' presence. Burned villages lay in their path and the ever-present signs of death, trademark of the Huns. Most of them, he could see, had not died easily. The Kushanites were a fierce and proud people and, even when surprised and outnumbered, they fought like devils. The women were damned near as mean as their men. They'd all been raised in a hostile land and each knew well the use of weapons. They'd learned in childhood. Evidence of their bravery was made clear to Casca and his men when they came across the corpse of a small boy no more than eight or ten years old. The boy's body had been trampled beneath the hooves of the Hunnish horses and yet, near his hand, was his lance. It was broken in two, the spear end lying a few feet away from the butt, with dried blood on its tip. The youngster had most likely set the butt in the ground and, when the Hun had rode over him, he'd speared him in the gut.

He hated leaving the bodies out there exposed, where they would be picked at by vultures and other animals, but he knew he didn't have time for the dead. Right now, he was more concerned with their living relatives and friends, fighting the Huns in Kushan. He knew the living needed him and his warriors more than their dead. They rode on. Three days passed.

They were nearing Kushan now, and several times his outriders had reported they had seen bands of foraging Huns, but in obeyance of his orders had hidden themselves and had made no attempt to engage them. Indemeer made the observation that if the Huns were ranging out this far, a one- and two-day march, they surely must be short of food and supplies. Could this mean that the city was still holding on, forcing the Huns to go in search of food around the countryside? Food that they expected to get easily in Kushan? It must be!

When Casca received word that the city was only a half-day march by foot, he called a halt. Making good use of the available cover, which was plentiful here, he ordered his men to conceal themselves. They were careful, using the pines and gulleys to hide themselves and their animals. Two of his junior officers, full of piss and vigor, impatiently asked as to why they were not going directly to the aid of the city they had ventured so many miles to save. This time Casca let Shirkin answer. The reason for this maneuver was similar to when he'd moved his forces to the other valley when they'd destroyed the Huns with the trick of suicide. Shirkin was a quick study and he'd use his brains instead of his emotions. He'd be a good general one day. "Answer the question, Shirkin!"

Shirkin informed the junior officers that it would be stupid to rush into battle before several things were done. First, they didn't know the disposition and condition of their enemy. How many were at the walls? How many were in the camps? Where were the locations of the Khans of the tribe? Also, our own men needed rest before going into battle; tired soldiers were ineffective and they'd suffer more casualties without rest. Shirkin ordered them both to return to their commands and think of the many reasons why the enemy should not be engaged today. He further ordered each to make a report to him before they broke camp the following morning. Indemeer and Casca nodded with approval. Shirkin was doing just fine.

This night, as was the case in the past five days, it was to be a cold camp. No fires on pain of death and Casca's wrath. Any sentry who fell asleep on duty would lose his head to the ax.

It was a restless camp that night. The anticipation of the morrow's events bothered all. Some would die, others would live. Many would be maimed and crippled forever. But such is war and the ways of it. Man's ultimate insanity, one for which there is no cure.

Throughout the night, the old-timers, warriors who'd seen much battle, passed on tricks and suggestions to the others who were going into battle for the first time. Giving them bits of advice that just might save their lives. The young ones listened carefully. Lucky charms and fetishes were brought out, amulets of all kinds. Though *Ahura-mazda* was the supreme deity of Persia, several men made offers to different gods. It couldn't hurt, could it? Wine was spilled on the earth to honor Zeus. A crippled horse was slaughtered for food and dedicated to Ares. These gods were holdovers from centuries of Greek rule and people did not lightly rid themselves of their gods or fears. It was always best to play it safe and there was safety in numbers.

Casca had no gods. He was not given even that small comfort. Though he still used their names in speech, from long practice, he didn't believe that Jupiter or Zeus were real any more than *Ahuramazda* was, or the evil one of the Persian gods, Ahriram.

About Jesus, he was unsure. The Jew had possessed powers, that was clear, but was he truly the Son of God? And if so, what God? Or, was Jesus some kind of evil spirit? Casca did believe that there was a force beyond his comprehension but exactly what it was he was sure he'd never know, even though he'd lived a dozen centuries or more. He did believe in the soul, the thing that lived on after the body was no more than an empty husk. Perhaps, as he'd heard from some devotees of different gods, the spirit lived on, waiting to be reborn again in a different body. Perhaps that was the way Jesus would return. He would have to keep his ears open. One day they would meet again, of that he had no doubt.

He put these thoughts behind, trying to concentrate on the battle ahead. But it was no use planning now, he needed more intelligence. That, he would have in the morning when his scouts returned with the disposition of the Huns and their movements. Until then, he would do better to get what little sleep he could. Rolling himself up in his saddle blanket, he slept under the clear, open sky. There would be no tent for him tonight. They were too close now and events could change things in a matter of seconds.

TEN

Jugotai looked out over the ramparts at the circling Huns, riding beneath their standards of yak tails and human skulls. They hadn't been strong enough to break into the city or mount its thirty-foot walls. But neither had the Kushanite forces the strength to drive them off. The time was near when a decision would be made either way.

He knew what the Huns were doing at all times. Reports of their activities came to him from his spies and scouts that slipped over the walls at night, returning the same way to inform him of their movements. A lot of them never returned from their nightly missions, but the Huns made it a practice to toss their heads back over the walls to let those inside know of their failure.

But a few were successful and had brought news to him of their coming disaster. The Huns were rounding up every villager, man, woman, and child, that could be taken alive, and were herding them into pens to use later. From what Jugotai had learned, they now had over forty thousand of his people in those pens out of sight over the nearest hill. Out of sight, yes. But not out of sound. He could hear them. God, could he hear them. Starving people have a sound all their own and it can shrivel the heart of the strongest warrior when he hears it multiplied a thousand times.

There was food enough in the walled city of Kushan to feed the people inside for another three weeks. Then, if relief did not come, either from their armies to the south, or from their Persian allies, he would have no choice but to go out and do battle and hope for the best. That hope, he knew, was slim, for they were outnumbered three to one. Even that was a lesser fear right now than the one the Huns had in store for them. They intended to drive the starving villagers to the walls of the city, give them ladders, and set them free to scale the walls.

Jugotai's problem was simple. If he allowed them to enter, they, in their vast numbers, would consume the food and supplies on hand so fast that their end would come in three days instead of three weeks. His other choice was to kill them. He shook his graying head, looking older than his fifty-two years. It was hard to consider killing your own people when all they wanted was bread for their children and water for themselves. He was also aware that if he ordered them shot down, he'd run short of spears and arrows to do the job, and again deplete his supply needed so badly against the Huns later. The Huns would come, he knew, when the starving thousands were swarming up the walls. Surely they would use that time to mount an attack of their own. Jugotai could not spread his men out to where they could handle forty thousand starving people and still beat the Huns back. No, his was a problem that had no answer. Perhaps it would be better to open the gates and have the entire city march out to die, at least it would be over with quickly.

A hand at his shoulder brought him around quickly. The handsome face of his warrior son, Shuvar, the pride of his life, stood beside him, bow in hand. He knew what terrible thoughts were plaguing his father and it hurt him to know that he could only offer the touch of his hand in consolation. But his father knew that it was Shuvar's way of telling him he was ready to do whatever his father said, trusting that it was the best they could do, even if it meant killing their own people. Yes, command was a lonely thing, but he was glad his son was back.

Shuvar had returned from Chin after an absence of two years. His mission to secure an alliance with the peoples behind the Great Wall had failed. His pleas had fallen on deaf ears. The nations of Chin were involved in a great struggle for power among themselves. One nation, one brother fighting another. They had no time, Shuvar had learned, for anything other than their own problems. Though they listened to him courteously, neither of the three kings would spare the men or equipment to mount a campaign to reduce the growing threat of the Huns. Each had told him to return when the wars were over and they would listen again.

Shuvar hadn't thought at the time that he'd live to return to them, and even if he did, he thought it would most likely be too late to do any good. The Huns had added tens of thousands of their standards in the last few years. They'd absorbed one tribe after another, turning them into partners. He'd returned to Kushan, sadly telling his father that they'd refused to listen. Jugotai had anticipated it and consoled him, praising his efforts.

Shuvar and his father, who still clung to the old style hair-dress of the warriors of his tribe, the Yueh-chih, the scalp lock reaching almost to mid-back, now gray with years, went silently down the stairs of stone that led to the streets of the city below. He knew they would, as was Jugotai's nightly custom, visit different quarters of the city. In every house, the inhabitants were doing what they could to aid the fighters on the ramparts. Arrows were being made. Bronze, copper, and iron were being gathered to take to the smelters to be turned into spear and arrow heads.

Every able-bodied man and stripling in the city took their turn on the wall. But still, it was not enough. Normally there would have been about twenty thousand living inside the walls of Kushan, now there were about thirty thousand. Refugees that had entered to escape the wrath of the Huns outside had swollen their numbers, but nearly all of these were women and children that would be of little use in battle. They only served to deplete their stock of food a little faster. There were not even dogs, cats, or rats to be seen on the streets; all had gone into the cooking pots.

Jugotai had fought against the wishes of some of the other commanders to have the horses slaughtered. True, they would help to feed the city for a few more days, but would leave them without mounts if they had to go out and fight, or go to the assistance of their rescuers, if they ever came. No, the horses were not to be slain, but he'd ordered all sick, lame, and old animals to be given to the people. The fighting animals were to be well looked after.

They passed the reclining figures of Buddha, the small smile on the lips of each patient, gentle effigy with all the time of stone on its side. Time to be patient with the follies of man.

Jugotai's old body held a touch of rheumatism from the years he'd spent in the saddle riding from one war to another. But his back was straight and no flab dangled from beneath his upper arms, as was common of men his age. They were still strong arms of sinew that could draw back a bow to the ear, sending its deadly shaft through an iron helmet and into the brain of an enemy warrior.

Jugotai was a warrior of a race of warriors, and he was determined to die as one. These problems of state and politics he wished he could leave to someone else, someone wiser than he. Jugotai was a man who enjoyed taking orders. Issue them and he would obey. But there were none here to rule. Kidara, the King, suffered from the dropping sickness, and his mind grew weaker and feebler by the day. His son, who should be making the decisions, was leading the armies to the south.

Shuvar interrupted his thoughts.

"Father, perhaps one of our messengers got through and relief is coming from Persia. Shapur is a tyrant, it's true, but he does need us to guard his eastern reaches. He cannot let us fall, Father. He has to send aid, or lose credibility with the other nations that have accepted him as overlord. Yes, Father, the Persians will come!"

Jugotai nodded his head in agreement.

"Yes, my son. But will they come in time? The hours of survival grow very small."

They entered the palace, acknowledging the salute of the guards. Passing through the stone halls, they entered Jugotai's office. Once it had served as the office of a man from Chin that had advised the king, Kidara III—Tsun-t'ai, a wise and gentle man who had been kind to Jugotai when he'd rode into Kushan with the Roman soldier, Casca.

Casca! He'd heard that Casca was serving the Great King in Persia now, but he must be very old. He had hoped to see the Roman again but it seemed that something was forever interfering with his going to him. Now it was not likely that they would ever meet again. He grinned, remembering that Shuvar had told him of meeting his old friend in the desert, and of him saving his life. But Shuvar had told him that the man looked not to be over thirty years of age. Impossible, but children think anyone over a certain age all look alike.

He and his son would eat their one meal of the day now, here in his office, in silence, together. A thin soup, made from the cracked bones of some animal, he knew not what. He didn't like to think about what it might be. Already he had heard rumors that the flesh of humans could be bought in the market.

Shuvar was worried about his father, but he was glad that the defense of the city was not his own, though he would have gladly taken the load from his father to himself if he could have.

He drained his bowl of thin soup quickly, it was

tasteless anyway. Well, he thought, if they were to die, then he could have no better sword companion by his side than Jugotai, Master of the Horse for the Kushanite Empire. Death will come when and where it will. The best they could do was to meet it as honorable men who'd done their duty and had been true to themselves and their oaths.

He excused himself, leaving his father to his thoughts, and went to see about his own men. They were guarding the section of the wall by the gate that opened to the road leading to the Kabul River, and on to the great Tarim basin and beyond.

Now, over the hill that Jugotai had been eyeing from the wall earlier, another warrior was taking his meal on horseback. It was Boguda, Touman of the clan of the White River. He was watching the captives his men had rounded up. There were women, children, and old men only. All men, and boys that were strong enough to pull a bow or swing a sword, had been slain. He would send no warriors to the wall, only the weak. Starving warriors might just turn around and fight.

Boguda was tall for one of his race. Even with his twisted legs, he stood nearly six feet tall. His strength was the pride of his tribe, and he used it freely. His favorite method of executing prisoners was snapping their necks. He would grab their heads between his hands, raising them from the ground, then shaking them until the bones cracked. Then, he would laugh and twist their heads in half a circle until they faced the rear, while crying out loudly to the unhearing corpses, "You will never have to worry about what comes at you from the rear now." The joke never failed to elicit a proper response of laughter from his warriors. Who ever said that Huns had no sense of humor?

The women begged for food for their babies, exposing their breasts, hoping one of the Hun warriors would exchange a piece of cheese or a crust of bread for their bodies.

But it was a futile gesture. The Huns took what they wanted and never paid for it. The women and young girls had been raped repeatedly. Any soldier who was not on duty was authorized by Boguda to have one at will.

Boguda watched from his position for a few minutes longer and ordered ten of the prisoners killed for making too much noise. He wanted quiet so he could think. A man needed peace to use his gray cells.

Tomorrow, he would send them to the walls. One way or another, the city would fall to him soon. If not tomorrow, then in a few more days at the most. He looked to the walls of the city. Soon, all that was inside would be his. He would have it all. There was enough wealth there to make him a major force that could buy the tribes that wavered and provide weapons made for them in the armories of Rome itself, when he got his hands on the gold inside the walls.

The Toumans and Ka-khans of the tribes thought him a fool for going against the walls of such a city. The Huns, they'd said, were horsemen and such a siege as this was not good for them. They had no machines to batter the gates and walls and, unless such a city fell rapidly, there would be nothing left to feed them or their horses.

But Boguda had laid his plans for the siege of

Kushan long before now. The city would fall, it would be his, and he would build a monument to himself inside it. A tower of the living bodies of those inside, then he'd cement them together inside it. A tower of victims!

By all the spirits of the water and fire, there would never be such a monument again. That one act alone would make people fear him. People who'd never seen a Hun would shake at his name. His name would be used to frighten small children into their mother's arms or maybe even as a curse to ward off evil.

His iron-seared face was flushed with the excitement of his own imagination. He would rally all the clans and ride over the face of the earth as a whirlwind of fire.

Boguda of the White River!

ELEVEN

Shortly before dawn, a commotion awoke Casca from his restless slumber. Rising, he slung on his sword and belt and turned to see what was going on.

A group of his infantrymen was approaching, their voices excited, their officers telling them to quiet down. Casca placed his hand on the hilt of his sword; a commander never knew what might be coming down.

He could make out other figures with them now in the dark, small ones that hobbled along being kicked by his men and beaten with spear shafts and the flat of their swords.

"Oho, what have we here? Some monkeys, or maybe apes?" The Hun prisoners were thrown down in front of him, to lie prostrate before him. He was informed by the senior officer present that four of them had been captured when they'd ridden into the camp area of the infantry unknowingly. They had immediately swarmed over the Huns, pulling them from their horses and tying them up. There had been six in all. The two others were now dead. His troops had lost two men in the short skirmish. One of the men had had his face eaten off by a Hunnish war horse. Casca winced at the thought.

Ordering the four prisoners to be dragged to their feet, he sent for Indemeer before interrogating them.

His graying General made his approach to their area on stiff legs, the leftovers of an almost forgotten wound. It acted up now and then when he was tired or cold, both of which conditions applied this morning.

He bowed to Casca. "I am here, Lord, what is the matter?"

Casca pointed to the four twisted-legged, mustachioed captives. "These are the matter, old one. They stupidly stumbled into the camp of our infantry and were taken. Remind me to give the men a bonus when this is over. They did a damned fine job at keeping these alive for us to interrogate."

Indemeer examined the semihumans with distaste. "Do you wish to have them put to torture first, Lord, so as to perhaps loosen their tongues a bit?"

Casca well understood the need for strenuous interrogation and was not adverse to roughing up a prisoner if necessary. After all, they may have the information that could save the lives of his men. He would be derelict in his duty if he did not do all that he could to acquire it, even if it meant dismantling the captives a piece at a time. He knew that he and his men would suffer no less a fate in their hands. They had no civilized rules of warfare and would not respect good treatment from he and his men; they would more likely consider it evidence of their captors' weakness. But, he decided, before he turned them over to the anxious torturers, he would first try another method.

He looked over his prisoners carefully, watching for something, anything that would set one apart from the others. He found it! The smallest of them had a cast on his left eye, a mark of cataract on the lens. That might do it! To these beasts, anything different was enough to make them taunt you. This one probably had had a hard time growing up in his tribe. To be different was to be an outcast, and, if they did permit you to live, you always caught all the shitty detail work in the tribe. Yes, he was the one!

Casca told his men to move the three others out of earshot but, he added, to keep them in a position to see all that went on.

He took the man and stood with him, scanning the figure of the shorter man. His skin was leatherlike, the nose sunken, the head fat and ugly. Even among his race, people notorious for ugliness, this one would be considered homely in the extreme. He was so wretched that Casca almost laughed aloud. The man looked like he'd been beaten with a wet squirrel or perhaps an ugly stick. He was reminded then of a joke he'd heard from a sailor in Byzantium some years before. The seaman had asked him if he knew the meaning of "badger ugly." The answer had been that when a man wakes up with a bad hangover and a strange woman is lying beside him with her head on his arm, then she rolls over and he gets a good look at her face—rather than take a chance on waking her up, he chews his arm off. That's badger ugly.

Casca wondered what the wife and children of

this man looked like, if he had any. Well, back to business.

He talked to the Hun, trying a couple of dialects before eliciting any response. Casca had the man's hands untied. As soon as they were free, he reached for Casca's throat, only to have his hand trapped by a scarred hand at his wrist.

Slowly, Casca applied pressure, increasing the force steadily. He could feel the bones starting to give before he lightened his grip and could tell by the look on the Hun's face that he was impressed. The Huns respected strength in any form and Casca's grip had left his hand numb except for a distant tingling.

He spat in the face of his captor. Casca wiped the thick drool from his cheek and smiled gently. "As you will, as you will."

He removed his small eating knife from his belt and fingered its razor thin edge.

I know you are a brave and tough warrior but now I am interested in seeing how well you'll perform as a eunuch."

The Hun's eyes rolled wildly. To be tortured or to die he had expected, but to have his manhood cut off scared the living shit out of him. Casca continued:

"After I remove your jewels I am going to eat them." He slid the thin blade across the man's cheekbone, slicing the skin minutely, leaving only a red line leaking through the dirty covering of his hide. Casca knew he was getting to the man, from the barely controllable shaking in the Hun's legs, now beginning to run up to his shoulders.

"Then, my nasty little friend, I am going to turn

you over to some of my men who have no taste at all. They will screw anything, even you. This they will do in front of your comrades. Then, after they have used you, I am going to have you separated from all your parts. First your hands, then your arms, feet and legs. One joint at a time, and each cut will be sealed with a red hot iron after it is severed, so you won't die too fast. After that, all your limbs will be taken and buried in different parts of the country so your spirit cannot be joined in the afterlife. Your soul will never find its way to your ancestors and it will roam the earth forever."

Casca felt a twinge somewhere inside him at the words, "roam the earth forever."

The Hun was beginning to break. He had no doubt that the scar-faced man would do exactly as he'd said. Casca watched him, knowing he was weakening.

"I know you. You are not really one with your brothers. They have never accepted you and you have been the butt of their jokes and laughter too many times."

From the Hun's expression, he knew he had struck home, correct in his analysis.

"What good will it do you to suffer for them? They will not sing your praises by their campfires. Your name will not be told in songs of bravery. No! You are going to die most horribly for nothing, or . . ." He paused for effect and to give him time to think a bit.

"Or, you can go away from here a rich man. Those over there," he pointed to the other three who were now giving his man some very dirty looks, "those three will never leave this camp alive. They will be unable to say anything to anyone, and

I will do to them what I told you I would do to you. Their spirits will not survive to harm you."

Casca removed his purse at his waist and held it before the Hun, shaking the bag. The sound of gold coins clinking was clear and loud. He hefted the bag. "Here, my little man, is life for you. Life! With this, you can buy any woman you desire. Here is more than you could ever receive from the sacking of the city as your part. You know that your Toumans will take it all for themselves, leaving you only scraps or leftovers. Why not take this now, and live? I only want you to tell me a few things that I shall find out later anyway."

The Hun licked his lips, torn between dread fear and avid greed. The tinkling of the gold had also reached the ears of his comrades. They didn't care for him anyway and now assumed that he had made a deal with the Persian commander. One of them looked straight at him and spat on the ground, thinking you could not trust one with the white eye, it was unlucky and a bad sign.

Casca's prisoner made up his mind when the other had spit in his direction. Now, for the first time, he spoke, his voice low and reedy.

"You will do as you promised and kill them? And I can have the gold and go free?"

Casca affirmed his agreement. "That is so." The small Hun licked his lips again, this time in pleasure.

"Then do it now. I must see them dead before I talk." Casca had not expected this, but a deal was a deal, and the Huns would have to be executed later anyway. He carried no prisoners on this mission. He gave the order and swords flashed, taking the heads from the three Huns, leaving the torsos to roll on the ground, hitting the dirt before the bodies knew they were dead. His man spoke again.

"The rest, do the rest. I must be sure that their spirits will not come after me."

Casca gave the word and the bodies were dismembered as he'd promised.

"It is done, now keep your end of the bargain or receive that which I promised you."

The Hun needed no further encouragement. He talked freely, telling Casca of the thousands of old men, women, and children that were to be sent to the walls of Kushan this very day. He, too, answered Casca's every question about the Hun forces and told him of their leader, Boguda. Casca had a feeling that he wouldn't like the man Boguda very much and hoped they would have a chance to face one another during the battle. Any Hun who could figure out a plan like the use of the captives against the wall was too dangerous to leave running freely around the countryside.

He questioned the Hun about his leader's appearance and what standard he rode under. Once the questioning was terminated, he handed the Hun the gold. Now that his deed was done, the Hun was as friendly as a puppy. He bowed and grinned at Casca, baring uneven ground-down teeth and foul-smelling gums.

"My horse, Lord. Can I have my horse now?" Casca shook his head. "I said nothing about a horse. If you want to go you will have to walk."

The Hun started to protest but was stopped by a back hand to his mouth. Casca turned him over to his soldiers and issued his orders.

"Take him to the edge of the camp and release him. He is not to be harmed. Make sure he heads in the opposite direction of the city."

Casca had kept his word, doing all he'd told the man he would do. But he knew that the man's being on foot was as good as a death warrant. Anyone who found him would kill him on the spot, taking what riches he had. With his twisted legs he could not cover much ground and it would not be long, Casca knew, before some Mongol or Tartar thief, or even a hungry nomad of the desert would find him and do him in. If the Kushanites found him, may his god help him.

Casca didn't like what he had had to order, but war was hell. Where had he heard that line before?

He called his officers together, telling them of the Hunnish plan.

"We ride now. Leave our baggage behind, without guards, we'll need every man and, if we fail, it won't matter who has the baggage trains. We damned sure won't need it. The infantry is to ride double with the cavalry. Have your men take turns with them so the horses won't be exhausted when we need them most. Now go to your men, we ride like hell."

Urgency rode with them now. They moved in battle formation, flankers out. They must hurry, but still must spare their mounts.

When the scouts came back in to report, they said that they had spotted the main Hun force less than three miles distant, and that they could see the walls of the city from the next rise. Casca called a halt and rode to the rise, looking down on the fields in front of Kushan.

There was a distance, he estimated, of about two and a half miles before they would reach the walled city. It was an easy downhill grade, which was good. It would aid their horses in the charge.

The Huns were laying back now, only a few bands making random sorties around the wall, firing off a few token arrows to keep the sentries on their toes and unable to relax. To the left, Casca could make out the holding pens where the villagers were being kept. From this distance they were no more than specks to the eye, but the movement of horsemen about them was easy to see in the clear high air.

He needed to let those in the city know that help had arrived and to give them some idea of his plan. He summoned Shirkin, whispered in his ear, and handed him a piece of parchment tied to a Hun arrow. Shirkin grinned and left in obedience. Casca ordered his forces to remain behind the rise and out of sight of the enemy.

Shirkin came back shortly, wearing the clothing and equipment of one of the Huns they'd slain that morning. He had been aware that his infantrymen had taken some as souvenirs. Instead of his own fine-blooded steed, Shirkin now rode one of the dead men's, a shorter and hairier pony than the stock that the Persians preferred. Casca had to admit, Shirkin damned sure made a fine-looking Hun. He wore a fur jacket over his tunic, a head cap of wild mountain sheepskin with the hairy side exposed, and pantaloons of horse leather stuffed into high boots at the top. He had put aside his own long curved sword and carried the short straight blade that had belonged to one of the captives. Casca would bet that somewhere in his infantry companies there was a pissed-off warrior who was certain he was to lose his souvenirs forever.

In Shirkin's hand he held one of the Hun's powerful bows made of laminated strips of horn and wood. Casca could see the parchment tied to one of his arrows.

Shirkin looked to Casca for permission to leave and was given it by a nod of his general's head. He rode around the base of the hill, avoiding the rise and being noticed too soon. He galloped his horse casually the short distance and joined a band of ten Huns who were firing off shots at the walls. He waved merrily to the others and set the arrow with the parchment attached onto the gut bowstring. Galloping still, and guiding his horse with his legs, he took careful aim at a spot close to what looked like a Kushanite officer. He loosed the arrow, missing the man's head less than ten inches, sinking it into a timber beside him. Shirkin yelled to the man, "Use your eyes or lose your head!" The fact that one of the Huns spoke a civilized tongue was enough to attract the man's attention if the arrow had not already made him duck for cover. He whirled his horse around and nonchalantly rode away from the walls, leaving the Huns to their sport and amusement. He'd done his job; now it was time to get his ass out while he still could.

Shirkin reported back to Casca after his ride.

"It is done, Lord, and I am sure they have your message. As I rode off, I saw one I took to be an officer pulling the arrow out of the beam I shot it into."

Casca was pleased and told Shirkin to change back into his own uniform before one of the men got excited and filled his young ass with arrows.

He called for Indemeer to summon his staff and he'd give them the battle plan. His idea had started taking shape when he'd seen the Huns start herding the captives out of the pens and toward the walls. In less than an hour it would make or break them.

As he waited for his officers, he watched the Hun force gathering in their strength. Forty thousand men of the steppes, circling each other, throwing up clouds of dust to rise with the wind. Shamans were casting spells to bring them luck and reading the signs of the earth and sky to ensure their victory and to please the god and spirits of battle. Boguda had ordered that a thousand women be sacrificed so that their blood could spill onto the earth and sink into the dry dust to feed the Great Mother.

Casca watched the slaughter of the women but could do nothing about it at the moment. It was too soon now to commit his men. If he charged at this moment all would be lost. But he sent word back to his men about what had happened to the women, and that if they failed this day, the Huns would be in Persia next, doing the same thing to their women. This day, there could be no mercy, for they surely would receive none from the Huns. They must have only one thing in mind, and that was to *kill, kill, kill!*

The Kushanite officer that Shirkin had nearly clipped with the shaft noticed the parchment attached to the arrow and pulled it from the timber, taking it to Shuvar, officer of the guard at the time. Shuvar read the message and smiled, double-timing off to locate his father. He finally found him looking over some wounded men, trying to decide which ones might still be able to return to the walls for their shift.

He was scarcely able to contain his excitement as

he pulled his father aside so none could hear and whispered:

"He is here!"

Jugotai responded somewhat testily. "Who is here, pup?"

"Father, Casca has come. Casca the Roman. He is leading a Persian relief force. Even now they are just out of our sight over the hills to the west. He says the time has come for us to meet again and we should come to him when the moment is right. We are to be ready and mounted at that moment, then everyone must attack at the same time, even the guards on the walls are to let themselves down by rope if necessary. He needs everyone, Father."

Jugotai jerked the message from his son's hand, reading it slowly. He wasn't very good at making out words, but his son was a fine reader. His eyes began to water, tears forming. "He is here. My old friend has come to help me once more. It is good that I shall see him again before I die."

Forcing back his emotions, he told Shuvar to do as the Roman had bade them. "Get them all ready, my son. The time will come soon, if I know my Roman friend."

After ordering his horse made ready for him and held at the bottom of the steps in mounting position, Jugotai went up to the wall to wait. Soon, he would ride out to meet his old friend and sword mate again.

TWELVE

The time was near. His men were positioned. The cavalry in two broad fronts, the infantry behind them, long lances in their hands. Many had spears that resembled gaffing hooks more than anything else. Casca had first seen them used in the forests of Germany, when the Teutonic tribesmen had used them to pull the young Equites from their horses and slit their throats before they could rise to fight.

The women and children, wailing and crying, were being savagely whipped by the Huns and herded to the walls. Any that fell along the way died in place. Babes were being trampled beneath the hooves of the warhorses to lie broken in the dust.

The captives reached the wall, crying and begging for mercy from those up on the ramparts. They carried with them the ladders, holding their babies in their arms as they stumbled and clumsily raised the ladders to lie against the stones of the city. They wailed and pleaded for those on the ramparts not to kill them, for they only wanted food for their babies, and themselves if there was enough.

"Food for our starving children," they cried. "Mercy, have mercy. Pity us and save our children."

The archers on the wall held their fire. The Huns were an equestrian cloud, circling the walls, waiting for the moment to make their own assault.

Casca gave the order and the horns of battle blared loud and long to echo across the valley floor. Once, then again, and his men moved forth. Slowly at first, then faster, gathering momentum, ten thousand of the finest warriors in the Persian army surged forth, an irresistible tide.

They rode even faster now, the beat of their horses' hooves pounding in time with their own pulses. Casca was in the lead of the element on the right. He'd chosen this position because, not only would it take him straight to the gate of the wall, where he was relying on Jugotai's exit, but it also put him in the vicinity of where he'd seen Boguda's standards. Casca carried one of the long lances grasped firmly to his side, letting the urge for battle take him. There would be no time for fine tactics of war today. It was plain. They were to break directly into them and kill relentlessly, until there were no more.

The infantry was doing its best to keep up with the rest of the troops, while, at the same time, obeying his orders not to wind themselves. He'd warned them to half walk and half run until they were near enough to the foray to form a square, then they would halt until ordered to move. They would form an island in the sea of battle, from which Casca's men would regroup and charge again.

He rode faster now, bent low over the mane of his steed. He could smell the acrid sweat from the lunging animal, hoping it wouldn't lose footing and fall in the charge.

They could see the faces of the individual Huns now, looming ever closer as they neared. The shock of surprise showed clearly in their eyes by this change of events; they were not prepared for this. It would take some time for them to reorganize for an attack and they clearly did not have time for that.

Casca cursed as his spear sank into the belly of a nomad and was twisted from his grasp. "Damn, Jugotai, come on out." The main Persian forces split the Huns into two disjointed fragments, then, whirling about and keeping the momentum of their charge going, they struck with everything they had. Horses screamed and men died, gasping for breath and not finding it.

Casca rode on, gritting his teeth, yelling silent orders to his old friend behind the walls.

"Now, Jugotai. Come out now!"

The Huns were rallying in force and beginning to repel the Persians. Casca rode through the ranks of the Huns, wildly swinging his blade like a cleaver. There was no time for any of the finesse of the arena now. He barely missed trampling a knot of terrified women and children. He whipped his horse into a turn and as it reared in fright, he screamed at the women and old men.

"Help us! Now is the time. Fight if you want to save yourselves and your babies. Take vengeance on these animals. Fight, damn you all. Fight!"

The women hesitated a moment, torn between fear of the Huns and indecision as to what to do. It was near panic all around, but suddenly, one woman handed her baby to an old crone and threw herself into the path of an oncoming Hun on horseback. She grabbed his reins and the horse stumbled, tossing its dwarfish master to the ground. That did it. The women broke, setting their children into the arms of the older women and aged men, or even on the ground if no one was there to receive them. They tore the downed Huns to pieces with their savage hands and untrimmed nails, and went immediately after more who'd been knocked from their mounts or thrown by their scared animals.

Casca wheeled his horse around, and kicking it in the flanks, urged it forward and through the mass of men, animals that had fallen, and wild vengeful females, to the other side of the circling Huns. Cut and battered, but still in the saddle, he rushed his sobbing animal to the safety of the square that had been formed by his arriving infantry. He rode through a gap they'd just opened in their ranks and gave them his orders.

"Advance one step at a time. Set your spears with the butts to the ground and aim for the horses' chests. If you kill the horses, the Huns will be nearly useless on the ground."

He charged out once more, content that his orders would be obeyed to the letter.

A trumpet came to him from the walls as the sound of the massive gate of iron and wood crashing down told him that Jugotai was coming. It seemed much longer to him, as well as to his soldiers, but the actual time that had elapsed since their first assault, had been only seven minutes. Yet, a lifetime for the hundreds that now lay dead.

Boguda tried to get his men into some sense of

order, but they were too confused. Where had all these Persians come from? He slashed open the face of an enraged woman and trampled her small child underhoof. The brat had tried to climb up into the saddle with him, screaming that she was going to kill the rider.

Boguda gathered a force around him and called to the other Toumans to restrain their men and attack as one.

As Boguda gave his orders, so did Jugotai give his. He and Shuvar led the throngs of the city as they all burst from the gates. He'd warned them that this was their last and only chance for survival, and they hit the Huns outside their walls like winds of death. Each resident of Kushan was determined and bound to take at least one Hun with him if he fell. They broke the Huns' flank and turned in on it to aid the Persians, who were now beginning to falter. They'd now lost the initial impetus of the charge, as the battle had been downgraded into ten thousand individual conflicts.

Most surprising to Shuvar was the vicious attack by the women. They were picking up weapons from dead warriors of both sides and doing deadly work against their enemy. They weren't experts at what they were doing but their hate made them as dangerous as any warrior. There was no stopping them now. Any Hun who fell and ended up in their hands, was more than lucky if he died swiftly. It seemed that the women were somehow finding time to pay them back for the rapings and killings.

Shuvar stayed close to his father's side. It was an honor to be with him in battle and if they were to die, then he would share the moment with the man he loved most in all the world. They rode at the head of their forces. They'd mustered nearly six thousand men that could sit upon a saddle. Those that didn't have horses were even now coming over the walls to join the women in their rage.

Many men saw women in a new light that day— not just feeble things waiting for their bellies to be filled by the seed of their mates, but as wrathful raging powers that hated as no man ever could.

The battle surged on, back and forth, but the square of infantry that Casca had ordered made the difference. The square advanced as he'd ordered, one step at a time all the way to the wall until they had split the forces of the Huns into parts that could be dealt with separately.

The superior discipline of the Persians began to tell. They reorganized faster and responded to a single will with more rapidity than the Huns could ever hope to master. Gradually, they began to gain control of the battle.

Jugotai waged war as if this might be his last battle. His blood boiled and the passion of the day overrode all else. For a time, youth came back to aged muscles and bones. He fought with a ferocity that left his son in open-mouthed awe of his father. They worked their way into the center of the gap held by the infantry and wheeled to slice into the left flank, rolling the Huns up into a massed, milling knot of blood-lusting savages, aware that they would have to win or die. This was a fight to the finish and it was known by all that the victor would show no mercy to the vanquished. They killed, both sides, the Huns crying aloud for their gods to give them strength to kill their enemies.

Casca was drenched with both his own blood and that of the Huns. His tunic was torn in a dozen places; all that had saved him thus far from even worse injury was the shirt of fine chain mail he wore beneath his green cotton outer garment. His sword was becoming dull from the repeated slashing against Hun shields.

The battle was beginning to get to him. He could feel what the Nordic tribes called the berserker rage gaining control of him and he fought it off, not wanting to lose that control. But he was unable to resist it. The berserker finally took complete charge of his sanity as he rode over the body of a ten-year-old that had been trampled by the hooves of Boguda's horse. The sight of the small bleeding body snapped the final restraints and he broke entirely.

He sobbed and cried, tears running freely down his scarred face, as he raced forward slashing and killing, then laughing hysterically. His sword reached endlessly for new bodies to drink in. He thirsted for blood, a berscrk slayer of the enemy, unable to be sated. Even his own men drew away, avoiding him in fear. They'd never seen anything like their commander, who would circle like a child in play, laughing wildly, then slash down on a foe, splitting him open from his brain casing to his chest, then crying out to the Huns to send him some more for he had yet to have his fill.

Jugotai spotted Casca. Even his blood-stained tunic and flinging arm and crying face had not hidden him from his Kushanite friend.

He kicked his mount in the flanks and tried to fight his way through to Casca's position. Huns were as close as lice on all sides and it seemed impossible to proceed more than a foot or two without getting slaughtered. Yet, inch by slow inch, he came closer to his old sword mate. Shuvar had been separated from his father, fighting desperately just to stay alive himself. He cut and thrust his blade, reaching out to pluck an eye out or dance across the throat of his opponent. He was an artist, picking his targets and conserving his strength by wasting no motion. But his father was away from him now and he could not get to his side. At least for the time being, he couldn't. Shuvar, too, had seen the scar-faced stranger who had saved him in the desert five years before, and knew that his father was trying to reach his old friend.

A loud cry brought Jugotai's head around. As he turned, a spear sank its full length into his leg, piercing through the other side and into the horse's side. The animal stumbled and threw Jugotai to the ground.

He called out, "Casca!"

The sound of Jugotai's voice broke through the blood mist surrounding Casca's mind, pulling him back from the slaughter.

Boguda was in a blind rage, aware that he was losing the battle and his glory that was to be. Victory was slipping through his fingers as his men kept falling and dying all around him. He knew his end was near and decided to go for it all. If he had to die, then he would take as many of them with him as possible. He spotted the leader of the Kushanites, Jugotai, and started toward him just as the chieftain with the graying ponytail fell to the ground. He managed his way through the melee, beating his horse with the flat of his sword. Nothing mattered now except to kill anyone or anything within reach, especially the leaders. Jugotai was directly in his path now as he bore down on him. The chief of the Kushanites, pinned beneath his horse but sitting up, raised his sword as Boguda struck downward. Boguda's eyes were wild with passion and he slashed at the chieftain in hatred. Jugotai was able to deflect the blade of Boguda just enough to ward off a killing blow, but still, the power of the blow broke through and Boguda's sword sunk into the side of his chest, slicing through to the rib and laying the chest cavity open to the extent that the lungs were exposed.

Casca had seen the blow from the Hun chief that had ripped Jugotai open and a cry of ancient primeval grief came from him. He still saw Jugotai as the young boy that he'd taken with him on the long trek years before. In his eyes the man was still a child. He screamed again and again. His horse faltered and he jumped from the animal before it fell, fighting his way on foot to where Jugotai lay. Boguda was involved with the killing of a young officer of the light lancers of the Persian cavalry and hadn't seen Casca approach through the melee.

His first indication that something was going on behind him was when he heard Casca cry out to the heavens in anguish. The sound sent shivers up his spine. Boguda had never heard anything like it. Wheeling his horse, he saw the Roman on his feet, standing over the body of the man he'd just sliced open. From the green cloth band around the stranger's steel helmet, he could tell that the man was a high-ranking officer of the Persian relief force. He bore down on Casca, trampling bodies beneath the already bloodstained hooves of his warhorse.

The stranger, instead of waiting in wide-eyed terror for his death from Boguda's hand, was throwing himself into the path of his horse. What was the fool doing? The onrushing animal crashed to its knees as Casca's sword rammed straight through the hide and flesh, piercing its heart. Blood was coming from its mouth and nostrils as it fell, yet it was trying to sink its yellow stained teeth into the face of the man who'd killed it.

Casca leapt deftly aside to avoid the last effort of the animal's teeth and grabbed the Hun by his tunic. He pulled him from the saddle and swung his sword with a blow that should have taken the Hun's head from his shoulders. Instead, it was met with an equal force that rattled his arm all the way up to his own shoulder. Boguda had squirmed his way from beneath his fallen horse and was under Casca, blocking his blow. The force of his counter was such that he'd knocked the Persian commander back on his heels, taking advantage of the respite to regain his footing. He stood, facing the Roman, his eyes flecked with blood rage and killer lust, his legs bowed like the weapon his men carried. Even with bowed legs he was still as tall as the man before him. His chest was barreled and his arms were long and knotted with stringy muscle. The two men squared off.

Casca moved first, a low lunge to the Hun's midriff. Boguda countered with a low sweeping blow that changed in mid-direction to go for his opponent's head, only to hit empty air.

They struck again and again only to find each blow countered. Both were master swordsmen and knew they'd found their equal. A dozen times each had tried to kill the other, only to fail and find himself standing with his sword singing in his hand and his wrist growing numb from the effort.

Finally, they stood back from each other, chests heaving from exhaustion, gasping for breath. The rest of the battle had moved away from them, leaving them alone in their own space. They would have it no other way. The two men warily watched each other. Not a word was being spoken, but the hate they both felt was as heavy as death itself.

They moved again. This time Boguda let loose his sword and grabbed the wrist of Casca, shaking the Roman's blade from his hand. They strained against each other, two titans locked in a titanic struggle that could have only one end.

Immobile, they held each other, their muscles and backs straining, the cords in their necks standing out like bands of steel. Face to face, body to body, they stood erect, each testing the strength of the other.

Casca was tiring, but so was Boguda. Casca heard Jugotai's voice coming from his rear. He listened but he did not turn away from his opponent.

"Put his head on my grave, Casca. Do that for me and all will be well." The voice was weakening with the effort.

Casca took a deep breath, drawing it into the depths of his already laboring lungs. He moved, using the strength he had built up on the galleys of Rome. He concentrated. But he could not move him.

By all the fords of heaven and hell, he thought, this is the strongest sonofabitch I have ever met.

Again they were face to face; Casca could smell his foul breath and the tepid odor of the man's body. This man in appearance was a damned animal. An almost forgotten memory came to him from somewhere in the distant past. "Use the other's strength against him. Have a mind like the moon. Use no emotion and you will conquer." Shiu Lao Tze, the ancient sage from beyond the Jade Gate, had said it many years before. He relaxed and let the strength of Boguda go to work for him.

The Hun suddenly made a strong effort to break Casca's grip. Lunging forward and expecting to find resistance, there was none. Casca rolled with him, drawing the Hun with him as he moved forward then; turning his body, he caught the Hun on his hip and slung him to the ground. Casca threw his body atop the Hun and wrapped his legs around his waist, beginning to squeeze. Degree by degree his thighs tightened, putting pressure on Boguda's lung cage. He was trying to squeeze the life out of the Hun warlord.

Boguda beat at Casca's face with his fists and fingernails, straining, pounding and clawing, now and then tearing pieces of skin off. Still, Casca squeezed. Calling on every ounce of remaining strength his legs tightened their grip and Boguda began to weaken. Feeling the ease of resistance, he kept the pressure on for a minute more, then shifted his position to the side, where he could get a grip on the Hun's head. He locked his arms around it and began to turn. The muscles in his back threatened to break out of the skin containing them, as he strained. He took a great breath and turned his body, giving his arms the aid of his back muscles. Boguda's head turned until he heard in his own mind a distant cracking that told him his neck was broken. He was not dead yet, he knew, but it would not be long in coming. Now he knew what his victims had experienced the many times he'd done the same. It was ironic that he should die this way. He almost smiled.

When Casca heard Boguda's neck snap, he knew it was over. He rose from the ground, holding the Hun's head between his own scarred hands, and raised the man's body from the prone. He cried loud for all to hear, especially Boguda's men.

"See and witness how the Hun dies, as shall ye all." Groaning and calling on reserve strength, he raised the limp-necked Hun from the ground and above his head. Holding him there, Casca turned and twisted, the bones in Boguda's neck grinding against each other as they moved into positions they'd never been in before. They were not designed to look backwards. His massive body was unable to give the death shudder so as to free his spirit, for Casca's hands had crushed his throat to such a degree that no air could escape. Casca let the body fall to the ground and picked up a fallen sword. The blade was so dull from battle with the shields that he was forced to hack at the neck until Boguda's head came free. He held the draining head above his own where the crowd could see. Then he yelled out loud.

"Your chief is dead."

The Huns broke. With their master dead, they resigned themselves to dying also. Their spirit was gone; there was no fight left in them, and die they did. Singly and in groups of a hundred or more, they died. The battle was lost with the death of their great chief, Boguda.

The forces of the Persians and Kushanites had joined. They were making a final sweep, bottling up the surviving Huns so that none could escape. The women were with them also. They had had a taste of blood and demanded full measure for what they'd suffered at the hands of the Huns. None were spared. The horse and yak-tailed standards were trodden into the earth to lie broken, ground into the blood of thousands.

Casca was drained and hurt. He left the body of Boguda to lie beside his horse that was still kicking its life away, and knelt beside Jugotai.

He started the task of removing the Kushanite chief from beneath his mount but was stopped by the groan of pain as he tried to lift the horse from Jugotai.

Jugotai, his face gray from the loss of blood, coughed through red foaming lips upon seeing the face of his old friend above him.

"Welcome and well met," he tried to laugh feebly. "It is as I thought. My son errs in his age estimates. For certainly you look much older than I do." He coughed again, grimacing with controlled pain.

Casca did look old now. His face was covered with grime and blood. Dust had formed in his hair, turning it a gray hue, and the deep creases of exhaustion and emotional strain had added many years to his appearance. He wasn't sure what

Jugotai had meant but he went along with him, for he did feel as if the weight of ages had rested on his shoulders and settled deep into his soul.

He watched the labored bloody breathing of his friend and knew that his minutes on this earth were not long now. Jugotai was dying. He covered the gaping wound in Jugotai's chest by tearing off a piece of his own tunic and placing it over the opening. This was the first time he'd watched an old friend die. Other friends had died, but not while he was with them. He had moved on before, never to return.

His voice cracked, dry from the battle, and he was forced to swallow several times to work up enough saliva so his words could be said.

"It is good to see you again, old friend. Our trails have been long, Jugotai, and I see you have achieved all that you'd wished for. When first we met, you were as thin as a rail and wanted only to return home to become a warrior and sire sons to fight the Huns. You have done well, for around you lie the bodies of Huns and your son is tall and strong. I envy you, old sword mate and comrade."

The descriptive words of *old* felt strange to his lips, because he still felt that Jugotai was the young lad he'd first met, though an old man lay beside him dying. A shadow fell over them from behind and Casca rose, sword in hand.

"Hold, Lord, it is only me, Shuvar, son of Jugotai. The battle is over, the Huns are finished. How is my father?"

Casca took the boy's hand, holding it in his own scarred and bloody paw. Jugotai himself answered the boy's question.

"My son, Shuvar, you are the light of my life and though my own spark will fade and leave, I know that I live on in you. You have made me very proud and have given meaning to the world for me. The ways of our people are such that we do not say the things we should before it is too late. Before my shade rides away from me I would tell you this. I love you!" The effort of speaking was draining Jugotai and his face started to smooth out with the coming of death.

The boy stood, his head to the sky. The Roman didn't feel the tears running down his face, washing the dust and blood from his cheeks and forming fallen drops on the stained ground.

Shuvar began to chant. Holding his sword above his head, he cried out in a strong voice, proud and with no trace of weakness, calling to the gods and spirits to take a warrior into their fold. He turned four times to face each of the winds and sang his father's song, telling the spirits of the air and mountains of his father's deeds. Clouds raced overhead, taking his words with them to the roof of the world. Shuvar sang, and all within hearing stopped what they were doing to listen. They knew a great man was leaving them.

Casca held Jugotai's hand and felt the coldness coming to claim him. As the life force ebbed, Jugotai's face slowly became the one Casca had first seen. The years washed away from the old man as his spirit let loose of its human shell. The moment of death was at hand as Jugotai smiled at the Roman above him.

"Casca, big nose. It is good to see you. I thought you were dead when those priests had captured you." His voice strengthened for a moment, as often it does when death is near the heart. His breath rattled in his chest as he choked on a piece of dried blood and spat it out. "We shall make it over the mountains and to my home yet, old friend." He was now reliving their last trip together, Casca knew.

"There is nothing to stop us now, the road is clear. I can see the high peaks where the gods live and they welcome us back to my homelands. We will always travel together as sword mates, won't we?"

Casca cried silently. He couldn't let Jugotai hear his sorrow. Jugotai shook his head and answered his own question.

"No! I forget that you have a longer road to follow than mine."

Shuvar continued his song, the words retelling every moment of Jugotai's glory for all to hear. He wanted to stop but he could not. The song must be sung as the soul departs. The time was *now!*

Jugotai raised his head as far up as he could, opening his mouth so as to let his spirit free. He called out the name from his youth that he'd loved best.

"Casca . . ."

The death rattle came with the word, the two of them as one. A single shudder Casca had seen a thousand times, but had never felt before as he did this one, escaped his lips, and the shade of Jugotai winged its way to the winds.

Shuvar's song stopped, there was silence over the battlefield. Then came the wailing of the women. They were not sure just who had died but the song was enough to blend their own grief into that of Shuvar's. They wailed and the surviving Hun prisoners shivered in fear.

Casca released Jugotai's hand, having to pry loose the old man's fingers.

With one hand he wiped the tears from his face and spoke softly to the still warm corpse below him.

"Come darkness, come peace. Welcome death!" He didn't know if the words were for Jugotai, for himself, or for both.

Shuvar touched Casca's shoulder and made a request that Casca honored. It was the son and the father's right.

Indemeer rode up with Shirkin, calling Casca aside to give him the after-action report. Casca told them to take care of the details and the wounded. He didn't want to stay here any longer; they would leave this day. The wounded would remain to be cared for by the Kushanites until they were well enough to return.

Once more, he rode away from the city, this time going to the west. Leading his army slowly, they began to climb back to the pass leading to the capital city of Persia. He stopped once briefly, on the hill from where they'd watched the Huns attack, and looked back at the walled city.

He knew what would be taking place below, even though he could not see clearly. The dark was coming now. He knew that four thousand Hun prisoners were being put to the sword, forced to kneel as teams of executioners decapitated them.

Shuvar's request was being honored and four thousand Huns would be laid in one massive grave, their heads between their hands. The Huns would be Jugotai's slaves in the afterlife.

Casca slowly moved his charger to a place a little higher and away from the weary line of his warriors winding their way to the pass and away from Kushan. The last red glow of the sun was barely visible on the horizon.

Quietly, under his breath, he said a prayer. The first real prayer he could ever remember making.

"Jesus, if you are the Son of God as You professed, and You do have the power of eternal life beyond, then hear me. Though by no choice of my own we are enemies, and You will not show me mercy or grant me peace, then so be it. But if You will, grant me this. Take the spirit of the one below, for he is a good man and deserves your peace that you promise."

Then, in spite of himself, he made one last personal plea, whispering.

"When will I have peace?"

The answer came with the rustling of the leaves on the trees. Gently, softly, words that only he could hear. This time he thought he heard a trace of sadness in the voice.

"When We Meet Again . . ."

THIRTEEN

Casca returned to Nev-Shapur, this time not participating in the triumphant entry with his troops. There had been too much sadness with this expedition and he was content to leave the glory of the victory to Indemeer and Shirkin, who'd served as his surrogates in the procession.

As the army was entering the main gates he went through the side entrance to make his report to the King. After he'd finished he asked permission to go home and was granted it.

Shapur, after Casca had made his report and left, sensed that something was amiss with his general, but he didn't push the issue. Rasheed, who'd sat in on the report, also commented on the fact that Shapur's Roman general looked a bit preoccupied and nervous. The King pushed the observation away. Rasheed always referred to Casca as the Roman and the King, even though he was aware Rasheed didn't like the Roman, wondered why. He had looked questioningly at the Roman's back as he'd left the court. Casca was different from the others. There was a quality to him that he couldn't put his finger on, and this bothered Shapur. The

King liked everything to fit into nice, neat niches. Shapur decided he'd have to keep an eye on his foreign general. He was becoming too successful.

Casca used the time to ease the pain of Jugotai's death, with the help of Anobia. He let Masuul go; he had grown tired of the constant bickering between the two. He had enough problems without being referee between his woman and his servant.

As he waited out the storms and rains of winter, there was another who was not idle like himself.

Rasheed! He never lost a chance to use the name of Casca in the presence of the King. Shapur was more than aware that his Vizier did not care for the Roman and was beginning to wonder why he sang his praises so often. But, Shapur said nothing about it to either of them. Shapur knew that one of his best weapons in the maintenance of power was the constant shuffle for position among his courtiers, and Rasheed's dislike for his Roman general just might prove useful in time. As long as they kept competing for his favor by keeping an eye on each other, his throne would be just that much more secure. Let Rasheed watch the Roman and he, Shapur, would watch Rasheed.

Meanwhile, Shapur's ears were fertile ground for the seeds of Rasheed's praise of Casca. He knew they'd bloom soon.

The King moved his court to the city of Koramshar, by the sea. He would spend some months there; it was good policy, he thought, for the court to be moved from time to time that his people might see and hear his judgments in person.

As the King's household followed him, so did Casca bring with him Anobia. They set up housekeeping in a small villa on a hill overlooking the baked walls of the city. There were tall trees around it, set in a garden that bloomed year round. Anobia was delighted with the place and showed her pleasure to Casca by trying to drain off every ounce of strength he possessed in the following days.

At unexpected times, she would throw herself on him, demanding that he make love to her. It happened at breakfast, at dinner, or even when he was currying his horse in the stable. Anyplace, anytime, was good and each period of sharing was as fresh as the first; fresh and new with wonder and surprise at the delights they found in each other.

The death of Jugotai, in distant Kushan, was fading with the months. Now he was just a fond memory that Casca would retain forever. For Casca, Jugotai would always be young; the gray-haired man he'd held in his arms in death was gone. That time was more distant now than when they had crossed the pass together. Jugotai had been no more than thirteen years of age.

Rasheed, too, waited, growing impatient for the justice he had been promised. The heretic, Casca, lived too well. Every breath that he drew was an abomination and an insult. The beast must be punished. He wondered at times if the Elder was not possibly growing too old for his responsibilities? Whose face lay behind the hood of the Elder? He'd find out when he was admitted to the Inner Circle. But he sadly recalled, that could not happen until one of the brothers died. Several of them were older than the Elder probably, and when one of them passed on to his greater glory, surely he, Rasheed, would have the opportunity to take his place and sit on the ruling council of the Brotherhood. There was a need for new thought and direction in the Brotherhood as far as he was concerned; it was growing stale. The Elder Dacort hadn't hesitated to treat the beast as he deserved. Now there was punishment if ever there was.

Rasheed was bitter and tired of waiting. He'd laid the groundwork for having the Roman swine punished by keeping Casca's name constantly in the ear of the King. Rasheed knew Shapur well, and the name of Casca constantly being brought to his attention would have an adverse effect on the King, turning praise to doubt sooner or later. He must now figure out the way, the proper justification for Shapur to make the final move himself. The King was ready, all he had to do was use the built-in paranoia of people in power, who see enemies in every shadow. Shapur would do the rest.

Rasheed, however, was frustrated and he cursed the Roman. He couldn't do anything more about it though until after the next conclave of the Brotherhood, and that was not to be held for another two weeks near the ruins of Babylon. Perhaps then the Elder might decide to act.

Time passed quickly and Rasheed, begging leave from the court of Shapur, rode to the conclave near Babylon.

In the ruins of an ancient ziggurat, perhaps, he thought, one the Jews had worked on, Rasheed shook the dust from his riding clothes and donned his hooded robe. He wished that the Brotherhood could meet in the same place each time and not have this constant moving from one site to another. But it was probably wiser to not have a physical temple and instead just rely on the spirit of their beliefs. This method did reduce the chances of their being found out, with nothing to risk save one day out of the year. Even then they sometimes missed a year or two if the way was too dangerous or the nations were at war with each other and restricting the members' travel.

No, this was more than likely the best way and hopefully tonight there would be a decision made about the Roman heretic.

He entered, passing the guards of the Brotherhood, and knowing that beneath their robes were weapons they would not hesitate to use if he failed to give the proper password. They were under orders to kill instantly if one did so.

The Brotherhood of the Lamb did not follow the preachings of weakness but instead heeded those of strength. These brothers would not go gently to the slaughter like those insipid weaklings who glorified themselves in the name of martyrs.

Rasheed could see that he was early. Several others were bringing up his rear and few were seated. He found his place as designated by his cult number and knelt on bony knees to pray until the time of the gathering was called to order.

Other silent figures came and took their places. Some of them he thought he knew as he occasionally caught a glimpse of a face under the hood or heard a somewhat familiar voice in hushed prayer. But it was not wise to look too close, as was intended. The less one knew, the less to be forced from one's lips under duress.

He let his mind fold in on itself, wrapped in his devotions and prayers. The age of the ruins of this Babylonian tower pressed down upon him. The great antiquity of the structure suited this meeting. As before, as at all the meetings of the Brotherhood, the chamber was lit by torches and lamps. One set of lamps was set to focus its light and show to best effect the Holy of All Holys, the Spear of Longinus.

It was an honored task to have in their care the most important relic in the world. They had guarded it for centuries. Only once had he, Rasheed, been permitted to touch it. The feel of the iron spear tip sent a chill through him that gave him a serene shiver to this day. The time he'd been permitted to touch the sacred spear had been when he'd been accepted into the fold, as had his father and his father before him.

Gradually the room filled with the sounds of breathing; all the seats were filled now except for three. Whether the three absent brothers were dead or circumstances had merely prevented their attendance, he didn't know. In the back of his mind, he wished that the three empty seats had been in the ranks of those set to the front, where the members of the Inner Circle were placed.

The Inner Circle! Twelve places reserved for the leaders of the Brotherhood and the thirteenth seat on the raised dais reserved for the Elder.

A rustle of robes caused Rasheed to raise his eyes. The Elder was standing before them and, for the thousandth time, Rasheed wondered of his identity.

Most of the brothers present were the leaders of

cells. Each cell consisted of twelve members and their leader. None of the brothers knew any of the others by face or name. The one sitting next to you might be your neighbor, or your master outside. A beggar might be a cell leader and hold the power of death over those that gave him alms for his beggar's bowl. This way, if they were ever found out and persecuted, the trail would stop at the cell leader. Some, like Rasheed, did not serve in a cell. These were ones in positions of power and influence. Some even held positions high in the church of the Christians, in Rome itself. These members were too valuable to risk having them betrayed by a cell member who might not be able to withstand questioning under torture, and their identities were even more secretly guarded. Still some had leaked in the past; there were always a few traitors who'd sell out for money.

The Elder clapped his long graceful hands together and convocation of the Brotherhood of The Lamb was called to order. It was time once more for the reenactment of the crucifixion. The elite of the Brotherhood had come as they were bidden, from the corners of the earth, to witness and participate in this most sacred of events.

The Elder, as was his charge, would now read from the Book of Izram, telling of the message given him by the laws he passed on to those who followed his teachings. Rasheed waited, as did the rest, to hear the words of Izram, the Thirteenth Disciple.

The Elder, his face as always in darkness, read from the scroll of parchment in his hands. The words were in the ancient tongue of Aramaic.

"Hear my brothers, the words of Izram and his message to us his followers, blessed be his name. We are the chosen ones, bound together as one in our great mission. This is The Word!"

Fully unrolling the scroll, he continued reading. He knew the words by heart, but it still thrilled the Elder to touch and read the scroll that had been written by their founder, Izram, over three hundred and fifty years before. His voice gained strength and he read.

"These are the words and the words I give you are true.

"I am Izram, son of Daniel of Damascus. Know ye that I have shared salt and bread at the table of The Master and have witnessed his miracles with my own eyes. Blessed be The Son of God! It has come to me to pass on the message and the truth about Jesus, his mission on earth and the road we must take to cause the events that will lead to his return. My name will not appear in the written word among the twelve who followed Jesus, for they knew not of me nor of my true purpose. Those calling themselves the disciples were only tools that were to serve their purpose and to be discarded when they were of no further purpose to the mission. Only I know the real truth, for it came to me from Jesus himself after his death. For then did I procure the Spear from the Romans. There were still faint traces of blood on the cold cruel metal when I first touched it. Then I, as Jesus had done, went into the desert for forty days, carrying with me the instrument of his death. There I fasted, taking neither food nor water, and waited for the words of our Lord to come to me. On the fortieth night, as I prayed, the words came to me. I touched the blade of the lance to my mouth and partook of the blood of Jesus and lo, the answers came and the voice of the beloved Jesus spake in the wilderness, and all that he wished came to me in less than a beat of the heart. Great is the power and the glory of 'The Living God.'

"Before I give you the word I received in the desert, there are things that must first be said, that you may know and understand the truth. First, I, Izram, knew that Jesus was not of the blood of the tribes of Judah. This proof was given in visions and through my studies of ancient scrolls that have been hidden from the eyes of the world for uncounted centuries.

"The bloodlines of Jesus came from the ancient and noble house of the Aryan peoples. His coming was foretold by the Magi of Persia long before the Hebrew prophets made their predictions. Indeed, the prophecy of the Hebrews came to them from the wisemen of the Magi in order to prepare the way for his coming. In Babylon, Nebuchadnezzar was instructed by his wise men to free the Hebrew slaves from their bondage that they could return to Judea; this was done in order that several families could be inserted into the Hebrew tribes that were of the Aryan stock and not Hebraic. These families were to be of the bloodlines that would lead to the birth of The King, as it was foretold in the stars a thousand years before it came to pass.

"The Magi knew that The Savior must be born in Judea for there would be a time when all the elements needed were correct and a confrontation would take place that would lead to a new world order. This was the true plan of Jesus as He gave me the word in the desert.

"Jesus preached love and mercy to the poor and the masses. That is true, for the masses outnumber, as do the poor, those in power. Thrones are built on the backs of the poor, not the rich. Jesus gained this support by promising eternal life to those that followed Him, and mercy to all that would accept Him. The other side of the sword was the use of fear, eternal punishment, and death for those who rejected His love.

"His disciples were to spread this word throughout the world, beginning in Judea, for there was where the confrontation would take place with the power of the world, Rome. The disciples were to bring to Jesus the masses, and when the time was right they would strike throughout the Roman Empire, loyal followers using the ways of death to eliminate those who stood in their path. A single dagger, properly placed, can do more good than a thousand warriors. We were to use fear and dissension to create a vaccuum of power, which would then be filled by our own people, and those who stood in our way were to perish. Fear is the greatest weapon. Fear of the unknown strikes the hearts of the bravest men and renders them weaklings by their own suspicions and natural distrust. We are to use this weapon under the veil of secrecy and only the true believers will know the real purpose behind what we do."

The Elder paused, looking out over the audience of his brothers. A sea of kneeling hooded figures, their knees numb by now, yet intent on the word of Izram coming from his, the Elder's, lips. He squinted in the flickering light of the torches, picking up where he'd left off.

"Before a new order can rise, there must first come a time of great troubles where the people are restless and the poor growing in discontent. There must be a conflict between great powers and distrust of everyone of everything. These times, then, are the waters in which our fish will swim and prosper. What we do on the days following this message are merely stones on the roads that lead to the second coming of our Lord, Jesus Christ. Our Savior! Our Savior! Not the Savior of the weak, nor of the Jews, for they were only tools to be thrown away when they could serve no more. As Jesus spake to me in my vision, it would be I, Izram, who would found the new order and pave the way for His return. When the world would be engulfed in turmoil and revolt, then would they turn to us for order, for we would be the only ones who could put an end to the turmoil that we alone had created. Afterwards, through Jesus, who would sit on the Throne of all the Kings on earth, we would rule for all time; a single power in which only the best and the strongest would rule under the guidance of The Son of God himself.

"But this great work was ruined by two actions. First, the turning over of Jesus to the Romans by the unspeakable Jews, who from this day forth shall be our mortal enemies, for they must never have a chance to betray Him again. And secondly, the deed of the Roman known as Casca Rufio Longinus. If he had not struck Jesus with the spear, then our Lord would not have given up His mortal body to return to His Father.

"I was returning to Judea from my home in Syria and was just outside Jerusalem when I heard word of the trial of Jesus and His punishment. I rushed to the scene but arrived too late, else I would have been able to save Him. For I had bought the services of a thousand armed men who could have easily overpowered the Roman guards and released Jesus.

"But the cursed Roman, Longinus, struck our Lord with his spear just as I approached and His blessed blood poured forth. There was a great storm raging and all had hidden their faces from the wind save me. I alone heard the words of The Lord as He spake to the killer, and He said:

" 'Soldier, you are content with what you are, then that you shall remain until we meet again.'

"Then Jesus died and I saw the Roman touch his hand to his lips and go into great agony, which I relished, and I knew that I was witnessing a miracle. The blood of The Lamb has great power. I knew that I had to have the instrument of our Lord's death and secretly arranged to buy it from a man of my own lands, a Syrian who'd exchanged the Roman's spear for another when the Roman had dropped it.

"I was downcast and full of misery as I went into the wastelands carrying with me the Spear. But in my vision, it came to me that the road is still open and all that must be done will be done. Jesus will return and from His words I knew that He had left the Roman for us to follow. Jesus said they will meet again. The Roman, Longinus, is the road that leads to Jesus and the Second Coming, and we shall follow the killer of God wherever he goes. He must never escape us, and when again he meets Jesus we shall be there to welcome our Lord. But this time, we shall have the power for Him to use. Instead of the ignorant and superstitious peasants as before, we shall have nations and armies to do His bidding and He shall lead us to the final great glory where it is paradise on earth and the worthy shall sit by His side in palaces of splendor forever. For He shall give us Eternal Life.

"Brethren, I leave you the Spear of Longinus for your care. Let nations die before you lose it. Remember and obey. Follow the Roman and damned be his name for all eternity. Glory to those that give him pain in this life.

"This is my word and The Word of God as given to me, Izram, the Thirteenth Disciple!"

The power of the story came over Rasheed as it always did and the final words of Izram ate at him. "Glory to those that give the Roman pain."

Nothing was said about Casca by the Elder and Rasheed was bitter. It was not until a member of their order was selected for participation in the reenactment of the crucifixion that he felt better.

The reenactment of the moments of Christ always gave him a great sense of peace and purpose, especially when the brother was nailed to the cross and it was raised in position. There he would repeat the final words of Jesus and another brother, dressed in the uniform of a Roman legionnaire, would take the Spear of Longinus and drive it into his side, that he might feel and rejoice in the pain that Jesus had felt, and through this act of dying by the very spear that had taken the life of The Son of God, the brother would be reborn to sit at the foot of The Master until the day of the Second Coming when they would all be reborn in His Glory.

The bitterness at the inaction of the Elder returned to Rasheed on his way back to the court. He could not understand why he hadn't ordered the punishment of Casca. The word was clear in the words of Izram. Glory to him who did!

Rasheed was not going to wait. He would create the conditions that would lead to the Roman's punishment and assure that he alone received credit for the deed. It would be a just punishment; he would make sure of that. It would exceed the pain given him by the Elder Dacort. He grinned as the wind whipped his face and robes. He knew the proper punishment to inflict and just how to have it finally done.

FOURTEEN

Events were changing the course of Persian affairs. Casca and his armies had been successful in eliminating all but a few bands of bandits in the mountains. All other resistance had been crushed.

But the success of the Persian armies in the field led others to watch them with suspicion. As long as Persia had problems with the Huns and a half-dozen other enemies, she was no threat to the eastern frontiers and provinces of Rome. Now there had been several small skirmishes between Persian and Roman patrols in various regions.

Rasheed continued to spread his disguised invective against Casca. Always in the most flowery of terms, but the message was clear: the Roman must go. Shapur, too, watched the progress of events. Astrologers read the portents of the heavens to him, and their message was clear also. He knew now what had to be done. There was a small sense of regret at the actions he must take, but the burden of rule was ever a heavy one, and so be it. In many ways, Shapur almost held a true fondness for the Roman, but that could not be allowed to interfere with the course of his destiny.

Rasheed smiled, his hands shaking with eagerness as Shapur put his signature and seal of office on the document before him. It was done! In two days, and after the King's dedication of the new temple of *Ahura-mazda,* Casca would be judged and condemned.

His work had finally borne fruit and now he would have the satisfaction he'd craved for these many years. Ever since he'd seen the Roman scum he'd known what had to be done, and finally it was to be accomplished.

Rasheed glowed with pleasure.

The morning of the dedication, Shapur wore his sword at his belt. A scarf covered his mouth that his breath would not contaminate the purity of the flames as his torch was lit by the *Mobed-mobedan.*

His back was straight, strong and proud; arched nose and dark eyes. His face a mixture of stern righteousness and pride. He looked every inch the part of a king today, warrior king of a race of warriors. His beard had been curled to lay in waves, cut straight at the bottom. His robes of purple and gold were set off with dangling tassels of silver. He was the King of Kings and the glory of his God.

Below the temple, every able-bodied man, woman, and child had come forth at his bidding from their fields and homes to witness the final conquest of things foreign. The Roman was noticeable by his absence. But this was not the time for foreigners, this was Persia for the Persians.

It would be soon; the red glow over the tops of the distant peaks gave warning of the birth of the new day and, for Shapur, a new era. He and his people had finally thrown off the yoke of the Greek Selucids and wrested power from the Aracids. When the founder of his house, Ardashir of Babek, overthrew Artavasdes, all of the Arascid line were put to death, save those few who had escaped to Armenia. Ardashir then had conquered and added to his realm the domains of Seitan, Merv, Khwarizam, Gorgon, Balkh, and Abarshar. The kings of Kushan, Makran, and Turan had come to make obeisance to the Persian and acknowledge his house as their overlord and master.

As the priests made ready for the welcoming of the sun, Shapur thought of his Roman general. He was going to regret the loss of Casca in more ways than one actually, but the time had come for him to go. Soon there would be another war. Rome!

Casca had served him well over the years, taking Shapur's armies against the Huns and rebellious tribesmen, and now Shapur's borders were secure for a time, and Casca had worked himself out of a job. His success in battle and his bravery had given him a great deal of popularity among his warriors, and that could prove dangerous to his King if allowed to grow. Many of the younger men of noble houses had vied for the privilege of serving in the Roman's command and all that a general needed for an uprising were loyal followers. Shapur would avoid that at all costs. But he would not easily forget the fair-haired and pale-eyed Roman, nor would the sly one, Rasheed.

The Vizier had cried loud and long the praises of Shapur's Roman. He had recounted at great lengths the deeds of the foreigner and how his men were growing in a loyalty to him that was second only to the King. Rasheed spoke in glowing terms how he was certain that Casca's armies would follow him anywhere and obey any order he gave to do battle with anyone.

Shapur was not fooled by Rasheed's words of praise. He knew that he hated the Roman but didn't know his reasons. He had noticed that when the Roman entered the room where his Vizier was present, venom dripped from Rasheed's lips, though the poison was honey-covered. But now, he agreed with the deviousness of his Vizier, it was time for the Roman to go. War clouds were gathering fast and dark.

Rome and Persia must try each other again and it would not do to have a Roman commanding Persian forces at such a time. True, he had told Casca that he would release him from his oath of fealty if the time should come that there was war with Rome again, but he could not let Casca go free. The Roman knew too much of the ways of Persia and the strength of her forces. He could take that information and lead Roman forces against him.

And now, from Rasheed, he had the reason he needed to sign Casca's death warrant and so he had. Rasheed had given him the perfect excuse and not even the warriors that had served his general so loyally could find fault with the judgment he would render today. He turned his attention back to the proceedings as a polite cough distracted him from his sad reflections on Casca.

The *Mobed-mobedan* handed him the *barsom*, a bundle of sacred twigs with which he would light the flame of eternity to welcome the sun on this, the longest day of the year.

He performed his priestly duties as the priest he was, Shapur II, *Shahan shah Eran ut an Eran,* the King of Kings of Iran and non-Iran.

The sun broke forth and the sacred flame was lit to burn eternally from this date forth to signify the supremacy of *Ahura-mazda* over the forces of Ahriman, represented by the powers of darkness and their servant.

"Casca," he thought as he touched the torch to flames. "Tomorrow, a new torch would be lit." It saddened him.

Casca was summoned to the court early in the morning, even before the cockcrow. He rubbed the sleep from his eyes and hastily dressed in uniform, ignoring Anobia's request that he return to bed and hold her. Once outside, he was somewhat surprised by the size of his escort. Normally there would have been no more than four or five troopers to escort him, but now there were two full squads. Twenty men meant he was receiving some special notice and the Roman wondered whether it boded ill or fair. No use thinking about it. He would find out soon enough, though he knew that he done nothing to arouse the King's ire and had served him faithfully.

Still, there was a growing feeling of apprehension as he rode to the palace. Once inside the grounds, the stone carvings of winged bulls and lions looked particularly menacing in the pre-dawn gray. His escort was silent on the trip. Not a word was spoken. Only the clatter of hooves on the paving stones of the street accompanied them. Casca felt a chill run up his spine. He dismounted and was led into the great halls, escorted by the Palace guards. His sword was taken from him before entering the main reception room where the King handed out judgments.

Inside, lining the walls, were many officers of the Imperial armies, but most important were the priests of *Ahura-mazda,* including the *Mobed.* Casca knew he was in trouble for sure, but still didn't know why.

Torches and braziers lit the scene, casting shadows long and dark into weird flickering pictures on the stone walls. Casca advanced to the prescribed distance from his King. Shapur was wearing full armor and holding his sword bared in his hand rather than the rod of justice. The sword meant he was dealing with a member of the military and as Casca was the only warrior in the center of the hall, he had no doubt that it was his ass that was in the sling.

Rasheed stood beside the King, the pleasure on his face as open and evident as was his hate. A flicker from a nearby bronze brazier bounced off a metal medallion on Rasheed's chest and Casca knew why. The medallion was in the spare, stylized form of a fish. Rasheed, he knew instantly, was a member of the Brotherhood of the Lamb.

Dawn was beginning to break over the city and the first light was seeping into the chamber. Casca understood the reason for his being summoned at this hour. The first light of day was the most holy time to the followers of *Ahura-mazda* and that was the moment when he was to be judged for some form of heresy. But why?

Shapur stood erect. Impressive, he waited for the precise moment when the light of the new sun would strike the prisoner. Then he spoke.

"You, Casca Longinus, who I took to my bosom and have shown great honor, have betrayed me and the Aryan peoples by treacherous plottings and the foulest of sacriligious practices. You have aligned yourself with the forces of darkness and have practiced the black arts. You are the tool of Rome. Rome, whose armies are even now preparing themselves to strike against us. But they shall be defeated and destroyed even as you shall be." Casca started to respond and was cut off by the wave of Shapur's sword. "You will not speak unless given permission." At his signal, Rasheed stepped forward. "My Vizier will give to the priests and the army, proof of this beast's dark powers and the pact he has made with evil, that none may say he has been unfairly judged."

Rasheed grinned, his thin face sweaty from the self-control he'd inflicted on himself in this moment of triumph. He left the raised dais and walked to Casca, the sound of his minister's robes rustling over the cold stones. He stopped in front of the Roman, snapped his fingers, and Casca's escort pinned his arms to his side. Rasheed took from the folds of his sleeves a long, thin razor-sharp dagger and held it high for all to see. Slowly, carefully, he slit the bindings that held Casca's coat of chain mail together and exposed the bare chest beneath. As a surgeon would, he laid the point of the knife on Casca's flesh. The metal of the polished blade felt like ice to him.

The *Mobed* and one of his acolytes joined

Rasheed to witness whatever it was that was to take place. The priest had the look of the fanatic about him, a full white beard and burning eyes that were strangers to compassion or mercy.

Rasheed forced the point into the flesh of Casca's bare chest. Slowly it sunk in until blood flowed freely. Casca said nothing nor did he make any expression of pain. He had felt pain a hundred times worse than that pinprick.

Rasheed then angled the edge of the blade downward slightly and began to draw the steel across his chest laying it open, a cut several inches long and about a half-inch deep.

Rasheed knew what would happen, as did Casca. Blood flowed freely for a moment down into the metal links of chain mail. Rasheed removed the knife from the wound. The bleeding had already stopped and the blood was clotted and dark.

Rasheed called for a basin of water. It was brought to him along with a clean white rag. The Vizier soaked the rag in the fluid and then washed the blood from Casca's chest, cleansing away the new scab from the cut. Casca closed his eyes. He knew what was going to happen.

The *Mobed-mobedan* and his assistant examined the spot where Rasheed had sliced into his chest. The *Mobedan* let out a low hissing sound between his teeth. The acolyte moved a brazier closer to them. The *Mobedan* looked again, then backed away, making a sign to ward off evil.

The *Mobed-mobedan* cried out, his voice thin, and wavering in barely controllable rage and hate, *"Evil . . . Evil!"*

The cut was already closed and turning pink, as both Casca and Rasheed knew it would. Shapur himself stepped forth to examine the evidence.

Venom dripped from his words. "Foul beast of darkness. You tried to trick me, but thanks to the wisdom and learning of Rasheed, he knew how to recognize the evil within you. You have proven your guilt. Let the priests make their judgment."

Casca said nothing. The shock of the rapid change of his circumstances had left him feeling lightheaded and numb. There was nothing he could do.

The priests conferred for a short moment and spoke into the ear of the King.

Shapur nodded his head in agreement and turned to the entire assembly to pronounce Casca's sentence.

"There is only one way that true evil can be destroyed, and that is by *fire*. You shall burn beast! Burn! And your ashes shall be spread into the wind. Take him! Let the judgment be carried out this very day, that he may have no time in which to make additional charms of evil against us. Burn him! Burn him, and do it now!"

Shapur returned to his throne and sat upon it, his hand pointing with the bared sword.

"I have spoken. Let it be done. . . ."

FIFTEEN

Casca was stunned by this unexpected turn of events. His mind hadn't really had time to register what had happened to him. Before he could voice any protest, he was surrounded by members of Shapur's Immortals, their lances aimed at his chest to restrain him while being chained, both hand and foot. A rope was tied about his neck and he was led from the hall. An escort of fifty Immortals were his companions as they left the palace and began the long walk to the square.

The reality of his sentence was beginning to register. *Burn!* I am to be burned. He had seen burnings in many places. He'd always thought that it was the most horrible of deaths. To be thrown to the beasts was bad enough, but at least it was quick and no comparison to the searing flames.

When they entered the streets, a drum began to beat, calling the people of the city forth to witness what was to be done. A court scribe, carrying the scroll that listed his offenses against the people, now joined their procession. He called out loud these offenses to the people as they marched forward to the place of execution.

Step by terrible step, he went on, the chains

dragging at his ankles as he walked. The mob gathered, the streets filled with leering faces, faces that mocked him and spat at him. Some were filled with expressions of religious fervor at seeing a heathen go to his just reward. Others bore the look of patriots who wanted this traitor punished for betraying their king. There were a few whose faces had the look of sexual excitement in their eyes, glassy and wet lipped. They were going to the burning to enjoy another's pain and suffering. He knew that they all, in their own ways, wanted him dead and individual motives didn't matter.

The abuse, filth, and spit being heaped on him as he stumbled his way forward, was familiar. Where had he seen the likes of this before? It came to him suddenly, and he thought of the irony of it. He tried to laugh, only to have it choked off by a jerk on his leash. *Jesus!* They'd done this same thing to Jesus as he walked to his crucifixion at Golgotha.

Is this to be my crucifixion? Jesus said that I must live until we meet again. Is He in the crowd somewhere, watching and waiting? Will he come forth just before they set the flames?

It was nearly three miles to the square reserved for special occasions such as this, occasions like festivals, parades, and state executions. A long three miles.

The crowd continued to grow as they walked, until finally becoming one giant, heaving organism. No individual faces now, but a mass mind that swarmed around him and his escort. A rock struck the side of his head and glanced off to hit the shoulder of the escort commander. The commander put an immediate end to the rock-throwing when he himself was hit. He bellowed out that all were to keep their distance. If anyone threw anything they would find their own heads on the road. This was, he said, by the command of the Great King. The torment eased; the only things being thrown at him now were invectives and curses.

The day was warming up as the sun rose. It was going to be a beautiful day, a fine day for any kind of celebration.

Casca didn't know it, but he was not to be alone in his suffering this day. Before he'd been summoned to the court, riders had gone forth across the Empire, carrying with them Shapur's written command. All that had served too closely with the Roman, or were suspected of loyalty to him, were to be put to the sword. This also had provided Rasheed the opportunity to include a few names of his enemies. Although he knew that they had never had any dealings with Casca, the opportunity to eliminate them was too good to pass up.

As for the Roman's woman, she was of no importance and would merely be driven from their domain back to her own savage lands in Armenia. Shapur also used the event to rid himself of those he thought might prove troublesome in the future. It was a perfect pretext. For the people would have no sympathy for treason or those that followed the ways of Ahriman. But, Shapur would have to admit, he had been stunned when Rasheed had made the cut on Casca's chest. The Roman was surely aligned with the spirits of the world. How else could he have healed the wound before their eyes, unless through sorcery? Rasheed, Shapur thought. That sly one. He had found out the Roman's secret and had been correct in his suspicions. Shapur was more than relieved that Casca had proved to be evil. It made all his decisions and actions proper and just.

Shapur and his court arrived at the site of the upcoming execution in advance of Casca. There, they took their ease beneath covered awnings and waited for the escort to appear with the condemned prisoner.

They had arrived! The place of death! Casca stumbled to his knees and was jerked back up by a strong, determined tug at his leash, strangling him for a moment. They pushed and prodded him to the center of the square. Everyone in the city had come to witness his punishment. The crowd was being held back by a line of soldiers, their spears held horizontally in front of them, forming a human barrier. Thirty thousand pairs of eyes watched his every move. Many of them were making signs to ward off the evil he carried with him. Some were touching lucky charms or talismans.

They stopped. The chains on him were growing hot from the rays of the now midday sun, beating down on him relentlessly. Sweat ran freely from him to drop on the ground. His mouth was dry, as if it had been stuffed with cotton. He winced as he saw the stake directly before him. It sat atop a newly constructed platform, six or seven feet above the ground. The instrument of his death! But, he thought, would it be his death? Perhaps even the curse on me cannot withstand being turned into ashes and scattered to the winds. Surely, not even the power of The Jew, Jesus, can reconstruct my body after such a thing is done. If that is the case, then maybe it will be worth it. Perhaps now I can stop my wanderings.

Shapur rose from his chair beneath the purple awning and spoke. Silence settled immediately over the crowd. As the King spoke, Casca could see that slaves were already beginning to pile bundles of dried wood around the base of the stake, shivering in spite of the heat of the day. Shapur's voice rose over the square as the audience hushed.

"Citizens of Persia, hear me. You have gathered here this day to witness justice being done to one who has been a traitor to me. One who has returned the honor and favor I have shown him by spreading the seeds of dissension and sedition. His perfidy and treason have been proven, as well as his worship of the dark forces of Ahriman as witnessed by your priests and holy men. He is the tool of Rome and the minions of darkness, sent to destroy all that we have labored to build and to allow the powers of the dark to come into our lands again." Shapur was excited and really getting into his stride now.

"And now, my people, his punishment has been set. The only way to destroy true evil is by the purification of fire. The light of the sun is pure and evil shrinks from its radiance. Now, we shall burn the evil from this traitor in our midst. This is my word, this is my law, and so it shall be!"

Casca was dragged without further ceremony to the steps leading up to the burning stake of green wood. The chains on his wrists were used to suspend his body from a spike set in the timber above his head. His arms were stretched out until it felt as if they would be pulled from their sockets at the shoulder. Only his toes reached the stones of the platform. The chains around his ankles were secured to the post to prevent him from kicking away any of the burning faggots when they were lit.

Rasheed asked for permission to speak to Casca before the flames were lit. Reluctantly, it was granted by Shapur. When he reached Casca's side, slaves were already soaking the bundles of dried wood with oil. Priests were walking the perimeter of the compound, waving incense braziers and chanting to drive away any evil that was still present.

Rasheed stepped close to Casca's face, looking straight into his eyes. So that the slaves could not understand, he spoke in Latin.

"Greetings, spawn of Baal. The blessings of the Brotherhood be with you this day. Surely and finally, you are about to receive just punishment for your sins against The Living God. I wanted you to know who it is who's responsible for the agony you are about to experience here at the stake. I only wish that it could last for many days." Hatred dripped from his words; his eyes narrowed and his face flushed with passion.

"Even this, as compared to what you did to our Lamb, is not adequate punishment, but it was the best I could do on such short notice. I leave you now to your fate." He came closer to Casca's face and spat in it.

"Burn, heretic. Burn!"

The faggots were lit by a slave as Rasheed descended, and the first tendrils of dark oily smoke began to rise from the wood at his feet.

Rasheed returned to his seat beside Shapur, whispering in the King's ear:

"I tried to give him a chance to confess his sins

and to ask for mercy of *Ahura-mazda*. But, Lord, he refused it and mocked you and our God. He said that the darkness would come and that he rejoiced in the evil he had done. He said his one regret was that he'd never had the opportunity to kill you."

Shapur's face turned beet red with anger as he spoke through clenched lips. "Then it is well that the heretic perishes in this manner."

The first tongues of flame licked at Casca's feet and legs, singeing the hairs. He bit back a yelp of pain at the touch of them. This was the beginning. He knew now that the pain would grow in earnest as the fire grew in size.

The flames reached up, licking at him, touching, caressing, then searing. Smoke rose in columns to swirl around the writhing figure tied to the post. He screamed as the fires ate through the surface layer of the skin of his legs and charred the raw tender meat beneath. The pain grew by degrees of agony until he thought he would lose his mind before the fires claimed him entirely.

A long tongue of oily fire slid up the side of his chest to his face and Casca felt the hair on his head ignite. He beat his head against the post, trying desperately to knock himself unconscious, anything to escape the hungry flames that danced around his body. The fire twisted with his every turn, eating away at his flesh, turning it into charred, black, smoking tissue and exposing raw nerve endings to the flames.

He recalled others he had seen burned and it came to him suddenly: there was a way to escape, not from the stake itself, but from the pain. He opened his mouth, pausing a bit for the screaming to stop, and inhaled deeply, sucking the smoke and fire into his lungs. The heat, reaching inside to the tender tissue of the lungs, caused great blisters to rise, then burst, with the immense heat. The smoke took the place of needed oxygen and mercifully, he passed out. No more feeling the pain of the hungry, consuming flames. Though his body continued to twist and jerk, it was only the nervous reaction of nerves and muscles being blistered and charred. Casca felt none of it.

He was out now, and unaware of the small man who had thrown himself on the platform and started kicking and throwing off the bundles of burning wood with his bare hands, ignoring the blistering of the skin.

Imhept was almost speared in the back by one of the Immortals, but the soldier's action was stopped by Shapur's upraised hand. The king called out, "Egyptian, why do you interfere with my justice?"

Imhept stopped his efforts for a moment and raised his own smoking hands to Shapur.

"King of Kings, you once said that I could ask a boon of you and that if it was in your power, you would grant it. I ask now for the body of this man."

Shapur realized that he had a problem facing him. He had, it was true, given his word to the Egyptian, and in public. But he had also issued punishment orders. He made up his mind.

"I will give you my answer in a moment." He turned his head to the side and spoke to one of the white-robed priests. The priest pulled up his robes and ran to the stake. Once there, he carefully studied the body, touching the charred chest and eyes, calling back to the king. "He is dead, Lord. The servant of Ahriman is dead."

The crowd roared with pleasure at his words. Shapur silenced them by raising his hand, palm up to the sky.

"As I have given you my word, Egyptian, you may have what remains of the heretic. I give you this favor only because I know that you are a good and righteous man without evil in your heart. But, before you claim the body, tell me your reason for wanting it."

Imhept bowed low from the platform. "Lord, it is for no other reason than that this man was once my friend. I know you say that he has done great evil and perhaps that is so, but in respect for the kindnesses that he once showed me, I would give him proper burial so his *Ka* could perhaps find peace."

The man's answer was no less than Shapur had expected. The Egyptian was almost as intelligent as he himself, though he might be an emotional fool as far as Shapur was concerned.

"So be it, scholar. You may have him." Shapur then addressed the rest of the audience. "These proceedings are now at an end. Let none interfere with the Egyptian and his professed wishes. This is my word, and so let it be."

Imhept carefully freed Casca's body from the chains, burning his fingers on the hot metal of the shackles. Several of the links had burned their way deeply into the seared flesh of the Roman, and had to be pried gently loose. He carefully examined the body for any spark of life, hoping that the priest may have been mistaken. There was none.

Shapur watched the proceedings for a moment.

It really made no difference to him what happened to the remains, as long as the traitor was dead. Even if the Roman was alive, he could now no longer be more than a crippled beast that could neither walk nor crawl. Already, he could see the legs were knotted into impossible positions as the tissue shriveled and drew the skin taut over the bones. The Roman's nose was not completely charred and the eyes and ears were still intact. The hair on his head though, was almost completely burned off. Shapur left the Egyptian to his corpse.

Imhept called out for one of his servants to come forth. The man listened to his master's words and quickly departed, leaving the stench of the smoking body to his master's nose. He returned in a few minutes, leading an ass with a carpet tied upon its back. They wrapped the body in the carpet, reloaded it on the ass, and made their exit from the city.

Imhept led the way to a cave near the sea, a place he'd found while on a tour of inspection for the King. It was not a pyramid or a royal tomb, but it would serve his purpose well enough. When he had the body unloaded and inside, he returned to the city to gather the things he'd need. When he returned to the cave, he dismissed his servant. The man left the scene, relieved, never again to return to Imhept's service.

Inside the cave, Imhept unwrapped Casca's body carefully. Peeling back the carpet slowly, he tried to hold back the rush of nausea that assailed him as pieces of blackened skin came loose with each touch.

In the manner of his ancestors, he treated the body for five days. He washed the shriveled thing gently, then bit by bit wrapped the body in long windings of linen soaked with oils and rare herbs. Unlike the usual custom of removing the brain by pulling it through the nostrils with long tweezerlike devices and placing it in a special container, in Casca's case he did not eviscerate the body. He was content to just use the wrappings, well soaked with oils, to protect what remained of the Roman.

He spent the next ten days in prayer, burning incense and carefully watching over the remains in his care. On the morning of the tenth day, he was finally finished with the ceremonial services. He'd done all he could do. He began to pile rocks around the remains. When this was finished he would seal the entrance to the cave to keep out scavengers, both human and animal.

Imhept tired easily from the effort of moving the heavy stones alone and his burned hands had not yet healed and were giving him some trouble. He sat resting beside the half-covered, mummy-wrapped corpse, his old body shaking with fatigue. Suddenly a rock moved under his hand. He thought he'd imagined it. Then another moved, and another. He was still trying to figure out if his mind was playing tricks on him when he heard a deep broken sigh from beneath the half finished tomb. Apprehensive and fearful, he put his ear closer to the stones and listened. The sound came again.

With trembling fingers, he started to remove the stones from the body beneath them. As the weight of the stones lessened from the chest of the corpse, the sounds of breathing were more pronounced.

Imhept removed the last of the rubble from around the linen-wrapped figure and saw clearly that the dead man was breathing. The bandages he'd placed around the mouth moved ever so slightly as Casca inhaled, then breathed out. Imhept placed his ear close to Casca's mouth and listened. He heard one word being repeated several times. Choking, whispery, and dry, yes—but clear and distinct.

"Hurt . . . hurt . . . I hurt."

He moistened the wrappings around the mouth with water from a jug beside him, then removed enough of the cloth covering the mouth to see the cracked, peeling, and charred lips. Gently, he used his fingers to pry the lips open and carefully poured a small measure of water into Casca's mouth. He moved closer to Casca's ear, whispering, "Do not fear, I am with you. I will take care of you. You will live."

Imhept left the cave an hour later, making his way back to the city, whipping the donkey into its fastest gait. He returned before nightfall, bringing medicines with him. He entered the confines of the cave and heard no sound. For a second he thought he had imagined it all, but then came the same long shallow breathing from the mummy at his feet.

The exhalation brought with it the same words that had driven Imhept to the city for medicines: "Pain . . ."

He removed a vial from his pack and carefully poured a draught, distilled from the yellow flowers of the highlands, into the seared maw.

For the next several weeks he stayed in constant attendance of his patient, spooning nearly equal portions of broth and opium down Casca's throat. He cleansed the body as well as he could, finally daring to remove the wrappings. His patient had slowly returned to full consciousness, for a few moments at a time at first, and then increasing in time spans, staying awake for hours at a stretch. Every movement that Casca made was one of agony. Imhept's deft fingers moved the cloth bindings from Casca bit by bit and, at times, pieces of charred flesh came away with the linens, often taking good flesh along with the bad.

It was three weeks before the last of the bandages could be removed. New pink skin showed fresh and moist where before there had only been seared tissue. Imhept had seen burn victims before but none had ever healed like this man. According to all knowledge, Casca should be irreversibly crippled and scarred, but his skin and damaged flesh was merely sloughing off, the heavy burn scars being replaced by new, pink, babylike skin. He knew he must be witnessing magic. Or perhaps a miracle. Were they not both one and the same?

Casca was awake during most of the healing process, and fully aware of what was happening to him. He knew that he was still not to be permitted to die. When the smoke at the stake had filled his lungs and he'd plunged into darkness, away from the pain, he'd been thankful in his last conscious thought. He'd believed that finally it was over. The end of his trials and tribulations had arrived and he was going to be permitted to die. He thought he'd finally beaten The Jew and that not even Jesus could put a man back together who had been turned into charred ashes. But now he knew that fate was against him. Imhept had interfered before the burning had been completed.

He said nothing of this to Imhept. He agreed

that his miraculous cure must have come about from the herbs and oils Imhept had used on the wrappings. It was lame reasoning, but Imhept didn't pursue the matter.

The first thing Casca had inquired of Imhept, when his senses had returned, was what had happened to Anobia? He told the Roman that the girl had gotten safely away and by now had reached her people. Casca was relieved. He didn't want her to be punished on his account. He was content that she probably thought him dead and wished her, and the man who was fortunate enough to claim her in the future, good fortune and good luck.

For some time, Casca was forced to go naked inside the cave. The touch of anything against his skin was like acid. But the skin began to thicken and soon he was able to even stand the light of the sun for short periods of time.

During most of this time, Imhept was ever at his side, leaving him only long enough to report to his superior. He made excuses to them for his absence, knowing that they were actually unnecessary. Most of them thought the little Egyptian was strange anyway and didn't really care where the man from the Nile went, or for what length of time, as long as his reports were sent in periodically, satisfying the bureaucratic processes.

Imhept was finally able to leave Casca alone and return fully to his duties. Still, he remained in the close vicinity of the cave and was able to check on his patient now and then.

For Imhept, everything was coming to an end at the same time. Soon, his contract with Shapur would expire and it would be time for him to return to where his real work was.

SIXTEEN

Casca stayed in the dark of the cave by the sea for four months, going out only at night to lie in the healing salt waters. Ever so gradually, the red, wrinkled skin sloughed off, first in flakes and then in strips, leaving new, bare, red tissue exposed. Hair and eyebrows returned to cover the bald patches of his scalp and brow. By the end of the third month, Casca resembled an oversized newborn babe more than he did a grown man.

Imhept was the only one who came to this desolate region and his visits were few. He came only often enough to bring fresh supplies.

Casca's strength had returned. He spent the days inside the cave exercising, stretching out the tight skin and twisting the muscles until flexibility and ease of movement returned to them. Often the sores on his hands would break open and bleed from the strain, but Casca knew they would heal fully in time. His wounds always did, the curse of it!

Imhept was astounded at his patient's recovery, but Casca told him nothing. The less Imhept knew of his capabilities the better. Let everyone find explanations that pleased them. From him, they would get nothing.

At last, Casca felt ready to go. For the last few weeks he had ventured out into the light of day for increasingly longer periods of time, letting his skin grow dark under the Arabian sun. As far as he could see, his one and only benefit from the burning was the fact that some of his lesser scars had come off with the dead skin, leaving the total carcass slightly less scarred on the whole.

Imhept agreed that it was time for Casca to strike out on his own. Every day that they spent in the land of the Great King was one of danger. He provided Casca with a sum of money, enough to provide him for some time to come if he was careful. Imhept had never had much use for money or wealth to any degree. Though he had acquired great amounts of it in his time, he never kept it for himself. He gave it instead to those that hungered, not only for bread but also for his kind of knowledge.

The last time Casca saw the Egyptian was as his thin frame jogged uncomfortably up and down on the back of the ass he used for transport. The two of them had disappeared from Casca's view and over a hill, heading back to Koramshar. As for Casca, he hitched his pack a bit higher on his shoulder, wincing a little as the straps rubbed his still tender skin, adjusted his sword belt, and struck out, heading west. He had a long way to go. He would again follow the old road along the banks of the Tigris and Euphrates and through what once was known as Babylonia, now known as Asuristan. He would follow the Euphrates past Firus Shapur until reaching the borders of Syria; then on to Calinicium, the first Roman city of any size, and from thence to Barbalissus. At that place, he would leave the river and strike out straight across the hundred odd miles to Antioch.

He wrapped his robes around him and adjusted the turban. Wearing this clothing and carrying his sword and spear, he looked to be no more than a lone wandering nomad, which was his actual intent.

But he still had over a hundred miles to go before he came to the twin rivers and could leave the nearest city to this place behind. He had no desire to enter the confines of Bisshapur. Casca wondered if the King himself knew exactly how many cities had been named after him.

He walked the first fifty miles, then decided to part with a portion of his hoard and purchased a spavined mare at a village near Biramkubad. It was true that the beast had not the strength nor grace nor the attractive appearance of the mounts of the Imperial stables, but it sure beat the hell out of walking every step over heated rocks and sand. As long as he didn't push the animal too hard, it would surely take him at least as far as the rivers, where he could perhaps arrange passage on a ship heading up river.

At Ahvaz he sold the horse and managed to book passage on a trader headed in his desired direction.

The boat was a shallow draft affair built of reeds, and had a single sail. Its only advantage was that it was light enough to use the favorable winds and sail upstream against the river.

Casca stayed to himself, avoiding any contact with the three crewmen other than to take his share of their meager meals of fish and millet. They, for their part, were content to leave their taciturn guest alone. If the fellow chose not to converse with them, then that was well enough. He had paid for that privilege, and he just might be one of the King's inspectors, out doing surveys on the rates charged for passenger services by the independent boatmen.

He stayed with the small craft until they'd by-passed the fabled city of Babylon, now no more than a deserted series of mounds and decaying ruins, showing little of her former glory.

Other eyes watched Casca's small craft as it sailed past the city. They were eyes that were hidden under a dark robe of homespun wool.

The Brotherhood was having a special meeting this night. A serious mistake had been barely prevented.

It must not have a chance to happen again.

Rasheed, head bowed, stood before the Elder of the Brotherhood of The Lamb. The rest of the Brethren, gathered here for this occasion, stood in two silent rows along the walls of the cavern, their faces hidden in the shadows of their hoods. They all wore the same rough homespun robes of brown wool, tied about the waist with a cord, from which suspended the sign of the fish.

Rasheed waited for the Elder's words. He was certain he would be promoted to the inner circle of the Brotherhood, for his accomplishments were great. Then there was the manner in which he'd had the bestial killer of the beloved Jesus punished for his sins.

The Elder sat upon a plain wooden curule chair. Behind him, hanging from leather straps, was the Holy of Holies, the Spear of Longinus, the instrument that had plunged unmercifully into the side of the living God, and had taken Him from this world before His work had been completed. The Elder himself was not pleased with the efforts of Rasheed and could show no emotion for the fool's error. If Casca had died, then the trail to Jesus could be lost *forever*. For had not Jesus said to the Roman, "As you are, so you shall remain until we meet again?" Surely this meant that one day the Roman would come face to face with the Messiah once more. He was the road. To punish the beast, as the Elder Dacort had done years before by cutting off his hand, that was one thing, but to turn the Roman into dust that could not move was plain stupid. They, the followers of the thirteenth disciple, Izram, must know patience and good judgment. Rasheed had exceeded his authority.

The Elder spoke softly, nearly whispering. "Brother Rasheed, I have decided how to honor you for your service. On the next holy day you shall be the one blessed, the one permitted to feel the pain and suffering of our Lord, Jesus Christ. As He did, you shall carry the cross and be placed upon it. Then, when the time is right, you shall experience the blessed agony of the Christ, and the Spear of Longinus will send you to join the others who have gone before you. You, as they, will sit at the foot of our Master."

Rasheed was ecstatic. This was a greater honor

than being admitted to the Inner Circle. He was to be one with Jesus. He wept tears of joy at this honor that was being bestowed upon him.

The Elder merely looked upon him as a fool, but this was the easiest way out of his quandary. Let the fool die.

Rasheed was taken from the chamber, escorted by two acolytes. At his signal, the rest of the Brotherhood filed out of the chamber, leaving the Elder alone.

His face still hidden by the folds of his hood, he sighed deeply. He was tired and old, and soon it would be time for another to take his place and continue his work.

He'd been frightened when he'd heard of Rasheed's actions, and for a time had thought they'd lost Casca. It had been the worst moment of his life. But now, all was well. The spawn of Satan was still alive. He was not lost to the Brotherhood.

The Elder wearily raised his aged body from his chair and pulled back the hood of his robe. His hands were delicate and finely shaped; the hands of an artist.

With the hood removed, the glow of the torches accented the weariness in his face. A young acolyte came to him; it was time for prayer.

Elder Imhept went to his knees on the stone floor and prayed before the altar of The Spear of Longinus.

SEVENTEEN

He left the boat shortly after passing Babylon and made his way further upriver. From this point on he avoided the company of others. He'd walked the last two hundred miles, his sandals kicking up puffs of dust to keep him company. At night, he would seek shelter wherever he could curl up out of sight and where he could protect his body from the elements. His face and body were ever hidden beneath his burnoose; there was always the chance that he might meet one who knew him on sight.

Each step took him closer to the boundaries of the Roman Empire and away from that of the Persians. Most of the distance yet to be crossed was arid and parched. It consisted of dry marsh beds where the mud caked and dried under the heat, cracking into a maze of interlocking clay fragments. God, how he hated the desert. It would be a long time before he ever set foot in dry lands again.

He saw the last Persian outpost and avoided it, taking a circuitous route around the town. He'd had enough of the Persians. What was it that the old merchant Samuel had said to him when he'd first set foot inside the walls of Nev-Shapur? "Persia was not for the likes of him." He laughed bitterly. Then where in the hell was there a place for him? Never had he found anyplace that he could call home, at least for any length of time. Always, it seemed, time and circumstances drove him on endlessly to someplace else where he knew he didn't really belong.

It had been thirty-three days from the time he left the shelter of the cave near Koramshar until he laid eyes on the first Roman city, lying below him now in a gentle valley. It was, he knew, Calinicium.

Before starting down, he stopped and looked back toward the direction from which he had come. His eyes reached far behind him, back over the lands of the Sassanid kings, Persia. . . .

From beneath the shelter of his hood, his remembering eyes visualized the faces of those he'd left behind. He saw the faces of friends and enemies alike. He was weary with the miles and years of his existence and wondered what would have happened if the Egyptian, Imhept, had not saved him from being completely consumed by the flames at the stake. If there had been nothing left of him but ashes and pieces of charred bone to be scattered over the earth, would he then have found peace? If so, then the pain of his burning would have been worth it all. But he hadn't burned and the Egyptian had saved him. Therefore, his way was open again, open to whatever the forces or gods of creation held in store for him.

One thing he knew—even with the prospect of true death, he would never allow himself to be burned again. It was too great a pain to bear.

He turned his face from the past and from Persia. In the valley below was his future. He heaved his pack straps up a little higher and started down the gentle slope to the first of the Roman cities on the Persian borders.

Involuntarily, his back straightened up, his stride lengthening into the mile-eating tread of the professional soldier.

It was late the next evening when a knock on his door brought Goldman up from where he'd been lying on his bed, his jacket off, reading. He was still tired from convention activities but had been unable to sleep since. Grunting with the effort, he rose to answer the repeated knocking.

"Just a minute, I'm coming."

He opened the door to find Landries standing in the hall, the manuscript in his hands. Without waiting to be invited inside, he entered and laid the story on the small round table in the corner of Goldman's suite. He helped himself to a glass of Goldman's Scotch and drank it down neat, making a slight face.

"That poor miserable bastard!"

Goldman agreed with Landries' statement. He had used the same description for Casca's predicament himself a couple of times in the past. Landries poured another.

"But what now, Julie? Where will he go next?"

Goldman picked up the manuscript and placed it inside his briefcase, smiling grimly at Landries.

"That's another story, Bob. Another story completely."

WHY WASTE YOUR PRECIOUS PENNIES ON GAS OR YOUR VALUABLE TIME ON LINE AT THE BOOKSTORE?

We will send you, FREE, our 28 page catalogue, filled with a wide range of Ace paperback titles—we've got something for every reader's pleasure.

Here's your chance to add to your personal library, with all the convenience of shopping by mail. There's no need to be without a book to enjoy—request your *free* catalogue today.

ACE BOOKS
P.O. Box 400, Kirkwood, N.Y. 13795

A-01

More Fiction Bestsellers From Ace Books!

☐ 14999	**THE DIVORCE** Robert P. Davis $3.25	
☐ 34231	**THE HOLLOW MEN** Sean Flannery $3.25	
☐ 55258	**THE MYRMIDON PROJECT** Chuck Scarborough & William Murray $3.25	
☐ 11128	**CLEANING HOUSE** Nancy Hayfield $2.50	
☐ 75418	**SCHOOL DAYS** Robert Hughes $3.25	
☐ 75018	**SATAN'S CHANCE** Alan Ross Shrader $3.25	
☐ 01027	**AGENT OUT OF PLACE** Irving Greenfield $3.25	
☐ 33835	**HIT AND RUN** Dave Klein $3.25	
☐ 88531	**WHISPER ON THE WATER** E. P. Murray $3.25	
☐ 80701	**TICKETS** Richard Brickner $3.25	
☐ 82419	**TRIANGLE** Teri White $3.25	

Available wherever paperbacks are sold or use this coupon.

ACE BOOKS
P.O. Box 400, Kirkwood, N.Y. 13795

Please send me the titles checked above. I enclose $_____.
Include $1.00 per copy for postage and handling. Send check or money order only. New York State residents please add sales tax.

NAME_____

ADDRESS_____

CITY_____STATE_____ZIP_____

A-02